MW00878501

M,
You enjoy
it and
always follow
your dreams!
-MJ

THE DEATH CALL

M.J. Logan

Copyright © 2017 by M.J. Logan
All rights reserved. No part of this book may be
reproduced, scanned, or distributed in any printed or
electronic form without permission.
First Edition: January 2017

ISBN: 1548229032
ISBN-13: 978-1548229030

Dedication

This book is dedicated to my family and friends, who have always supported me along the way and told me to keep on going! Also to my most amazing and loving mom. Once she published her book, I knew I could do it. Love you! To any young writers out there, don't stop! Let your ideas flow and see where they take you! Don't stop believing in yourself.

Lastly, this book is dedicated to myself. You did it Malia! You made your dreams come true, now go accomplish more! – M.J.

THE BEGINNING

Hello there. It's Melissa Logan here. I'm telling you now that this is a true story and if you don't want to get heartbroken or teary or scared or whatever, I would put this book down. In case you aren't sure whether or not **to** put this book down, here's a quick summary of the story. This is a story about my friends and I try to stop a curse from destroying our school. Now, let's meet some of our characters, shall we?

First up, me. I'm 12 in 7th grade with 2 brothers, my dad and my mom, but she's never around. Love reading and writing but hate learning about it. Next up, my friend Faye. She is one of my best friends and has been with me through all of the hard times. Kennedy, best friend who is a drama, dance, and musical theater lover. So funny and mischievous. Other friend Belle, really smart and is always there for me. My friend Amber, been with me since 3rd grade and is a crazy lunatic. Other friend Lucy, really humble and sweet. The last character that you need to know for right now is Ms. Genie. All you need to know is that she's my principal and only four words describe this woman. **She is a devil.** Now, let's start this story off were it all began, the day it all happened...

Thursday, March 8, 2018.
Right after recess and minutes before Math class.

"Okay. I bet you anything that Riley is going to drive Mr. Logan insane today in Math class!" Kennedy said excitedly as we jogged and panted into the middle school hallway with everyone else. We were panting because Bruce, this "creature" that Ms. Genie uses during recess to guard the boundaries of the school building, almost caught us.

"No way! I bet you 50 cents that it's going to be Stefanie! She and Mr. Logan are like fire and ice!" Lacey giggled as she got to her locker to fetch her stuff. I laughed and lightly nudged her in her side as I got my stuff as well.

"Let's just hope that we have a good class, whatever happens. It better not be so good that I think it's a 1st grader's birthday party. Like that ever happens anyway." I replied assuredly as I stood in line and gazed at the 8th graders jitter into their classrooms.

"Of course it never happens," Eleanor giggled, "Mr. Logan is basically the creator of funny! I'm pretty sure that's where you got your humor! If he doesn't live up to expectations, you scold at him!" I nodded in agreement. Without warning, I heard someone skipping rapidly behind me. I turned around just in time to be ran into by my wonderful boyfriend, Jeremiah. I laugh and he smiles widely back at me. Kennedy and Lacey start to "oh and ahh" at us but stopped when I jabbed them in the ribs with my elbow.

Jeremiah Baldwin. Has been at this school since 3rd grade and we have been really good friends until now. At the beginning of 6th grade he asked me out on a date and after that we were officially boyfriend and girlfriend and one of the cutest couples in our grade and the cutest couple in the school. Some people think our love is a little weird, but for right now, all I know is that I love him and he loves me.

"Hey Melissa," Jeremiah breathed as he hugged me with one hand and regained his energy. I hug him back and secretly rub his back. I let go and smirked at him.

"Hey Jere! Nice to see you again," I acknowledged calmly, even though I'm probably blushing all over. Everyone calls him by his name, Jeremiah. But I made up a special name that I first called him on our first date, Jere. That name is now a name that just we as a couple share and only I say. He smirks and sneaks his hand in mine.

Just then, we saw Mr. Logan himself step into the hallway and greeted us with a smile and a 7 page packet for the do now. As we passed my dad and were handed the packet, my dad stared at Jere and I with loads of concern, but I just quietly chuckled and continued into the classroom. He put Jere and I together as everyday math partners and sat us next to each other, so it's not our fault if we grin at each other in class. We then proceeded to have a 75-minute class of entertainment, torture, and learning the obvious concept of mathematics. The rest of the day was bittersweet, as it always is. You can't expect more with the hard working Mr. Griffin as our L.A teacher, the annoying

Ms. Caldwell as our Spanish teacher, the strict Mr. Blackwood as our Social Studies teacher, and of course our just cruel science teacher, Mr. Kennicott.

"Earlier in Math, what was my dad talking about again? Was busy thinking about other stuff," I mumbled as I walked with Lila towards our elective classes for the day.

"Oh Melissa! He was talking about today's announcement. All students must be picked up by car in the gym. No more walking or biking home. Mrs. Genie said so," Lila explained as she walked on to enter her class.

Mrs. Genie.

I swear she is one of the prettiest ladies I've ever seen. But I also swear that she is pure disaster and evilness swims and eats at her insides. A quote from Taylor Swift, "Darling I'm a nightmare dressed like a daydream." I always feel like she's up to something and that's she's always keeping her careful eye on me, just me. This is why no one gets in trouble, ever. One, she's way too pretty to mess with. Her prettiness gets into you and you're hypnotized against your will! Two, her office is a combination of your greatest nightmare and her torture playground. I shook away the thought as I continued to walk into the gym for my basketball elective. After a grueling boy vs. girl basketball game, 46-2 (girls won), it was finally time to pack up and go home.

"I wonder what all this "leaving the school from the gym" is about," Kennedy explained to Lila,

Jere, and I as the four of us fought through the tight middle school hallway, packed with middle schoolers.

"I just hope that we all even <u>get</u> home. Mrs. Genie is always up to something, or as she calls it, 'new ideas', " Lila added as we raced each other to get to the gym in time and weaved through picky 2nd graders and grumpy 4th graders. As we entered the gym, there was a section reserved for each grade and 1 expectation that was simple yet just plain awful. ***Sit quietly and wait to be called to your car to go home.*** Now, let's pause the story for a second. You would probably ask, what is the big deal? This is just a normal school with no problems or any curse but our horrifying principal, but no. This is just the part where all crazy things start to occur.

It has been 25 long, boring minutes, and surprisingly, almost all the kids were gone. But out of nowhere, only Charles Bronstein was called to leave and go home. Kids are usually called in groups since multiple cars can be outside at a time, but I really didn't care that for once only one kid was called. The Middle School section was right near one of the doors exiting the gym, so I decided out of pure boredom to peek outside so I can see the cars. But there were no cars, at all. All I could see was the empty street and the deserted playground beyond it.

"Stefanie! Come here!" I whispered urgently. Stefanie dropped her thick book at the sound of her name and hustled over to peer over my shoulder as the long bang from her book echoed off the walls. Her mouth slowly formed into a wide 0, a mixture of bewilderment and interest as her eyes locked onto

the open scenery. She frowned and turned towards today's leader of the Middle School area,
Ms. Caldwell.

"Ms. Caldwell! Why did you call Charles Bronstein outside? There are no cars outside and I'm pretty sure that he wasn't planning on walking home," Stefanie explained sarcastically. Charles started towards the door but assuming by the look of his face, was probably also wondering why there are no cars outside and he's still going out there.

"Stefanie! Follow the expectations, please. Last time I checked, you are not in charge. Charles, go outside. Your ride is waiting for you." Ms. Caldwell retorted as she quickly walked to Charles and hastened him out the door.

I looked back at Rosetta and Stefanie and we raced after Charles for simple entertainment and curiosity. The door was instantly pulled shut after Charles went through, and the door wouldn't budge. We peered through the slanted door window that overlooked a stretch of the street and the playground, amazed by what we saw. Charles was slowly wandering towards the swings, swaying side to side. His eyes, they were ghastly and his pupils were wide with what looked like confusion and fear. When he got to the swings, he gently dropped his backpack and lunch bag, leaping on the swing and starting to softly swing. As he got higher, it kinda looked like he was starting to fade away, his features blending into the sky behind him. By the time he got the highest he could possibly get on the swing, he had vanished from the seat, into the sky. I couldn't believe it, and I definitely didn't understand it any of it either.

"Girls," a charming voice chirped, forcing us to postpone our longing gaze. We turned around to see Mrs. Genie staring at us with her pretty smile that I swear was filled with complete madness.

"Go sit down and follow the expectations please," Mrs. Genie continued, "and Melissa? Your father is waiting for you and your brothers in his classroom." She smiled a little too kindly as she strolled out of the hushed gym. I gathered my stuff, called out to Marvin and Gale, my brothers, and quickly walked out of the gym. As we dragged ourselves down the hallway, Mr. Kennicott started barking out names for the next batch of kids whose rides were here. I stopped and glanced out the hallway window and there were a numbers of cars packed down the street! I shuddered as my brothers and I rushed down to our dad's classroom.

"Sweet pea! Boys! How was everyone's day? What about that new pickup system?" my dad Marco said excitedly as we walked into his messy but nice math classroom. He stabbed at his computer keyboard at his desk, and did it quickly, like he was trying to murder his computer instead of finishing tomorrow's assignment in Math. My brothers barely acknowledged him and as they walked to the seats near the whiteboard started chatting amongst themselves. I instead sat next to my dad and talked to him about the wonderful events of my crazy day.

"My day was fine, I guess. Math was hilarious, as always. But the new pickup system was pretty creepy. It was the same as pickup used to be, except there was a lot more people. But for one batch of kids, they only called this one kid from 4th grade, Charles Bronstein? He walked outside and there were no cars. Then he started swinging and then he just disappeared in thin air." I replied, using hand motions to really bring alive the moment, although I didn't feel like experiencing that particular moment again. My dad smiled weirdly as he packed up his computer and his piles of worksheets and packets to grade.

"Great story Melissa. Really, amazing imagination! Now, let's go home and our first job is homework," he requested as the four of us headed out the door and down the empty hallway.

As I tried to go to sleep later that night, I tried to forget about Charles. *Charles is coming back to school tomorrow*, I thought. When I finally fell asleep, I did believe myself. But I guess I was wrong. Apparently, it was about to get a lot worse.

T#E NEXT MORNING...

Friday, March 9, 2018. 6:02 in the morning.

Quiet. So quiet. I was woken only by the sounds of my brilliant ideas, the thoughts for the day, and my extremely annoying alarm clock. Tumbling out of bed and picking out my outfit (a brown diamond dress, a jean jacket, and brown boots), I decided to turn on the news on my miniature TV. Hearing the first few words of the news reporter immediately made me want to turn the TV off and go back to bed at once.

"Goooood morning Denver! It is a beautiful Friday in March with a high of 75 degrees and a low of 48 degrees. We start out today with a very interesting murder case, one with no evidence or body. Last night a child, Charles Bronstein, was apparently murdered after a day of school at Foxborough Elementary & Middle School. Although there is no body or evidence…"

I tried to think so hard that it wasn't true, but it was. I was there. I watched it happen. But now the question is, how is it all true? All Charles did was somehow disappear in thin air. Nobody killed him, right? Who said he was even dead at all?

I quickly got ready and rushed downstairs, rapidly making a toasted bagel with jam. I rush past my brothers, told my dad I'm walking to school, and ran out the door seconds later. I sped across the street to Rosetta's house to take her to school with me.

"No way! Seriously? I can't believe it, especially the murder part. All he did was disappear, right?" Rosetta remembered as we entered the school building. I was about to answer when someone grabbed Rosetta and I by the shoulders and pulled us back into the front office. These crab claws then spun us around to face Mrs. Genie herself.

"Ladies! What's the gossip today?" Mrs. Genie lightly snarled as she stared at Rosetta and I. I really, really wanted to smack her, but my gut stopped me just before my hand was lifted.

"We were talking about what was on the news this morning, Ms. Genie," I muttered, gradually getting my heartbeat back to a normal level.

"Oh! Today's news. I was watching that earlier this morning as well. That means you heard about Bronstein, Charles Bronstein? I think he's a 4th grader. It's so terribly sad, what happened. I guess we all have to pass, don't we? That's life," Mrs. Genie chuckled as she patted us on our shoulders and started walking back to her office.

"Better get to your lockers, girls. Don't want to be late for your first class," Mrs. Genie added as her evil nonsense faded away. Rosetta and I nodded in agreement to Mrs. Genie's point and ran to our lockers and then straight to class.

After 3 hours and 15 minutes of Ms. Caldwell, Mr. Griffin, and my dad's teaching, it was finally lunch and recess hour. Recess and lunch is a whole other playing field than inside the school building and the classrooms. Mrs. Genie isn't around to threaten you or just creep you out, but there are definitely other things to worry about. Boys, girls, rumors, gossip, and a whole situation of where anyone can hurt you or lift you up. This is a very similar version to The Hunger Games. You enter the playing field with bunches of kids, and if you aren't careful or stay with your crowd, there could be someone getting hurt or "dying". Then of course there is the "creature" that almost caught me yesterday, which we all call Bruce, due to the fact that whenever he roars, he basically says "bruce". As I quickly ate my chicken alfredo for lunch, all around me was the talk of Charles Bronstein.

"I just can't believe it, that's really scary to witness. Whatever happened, I'm sorry you had to watch it Melissa," Amber said through mouthfuls of pineapple. I nodded and as I swallowed my food and much more down my throat as I realized something.

"Amber, Jere, remember when we were in 3rd grade, and we made up a game where we were saving people like Charles when things like yesterday happen? At the end of 3rd grade, we promised each other that we would still remember it and maybe play it again?" I asked, my realization tone getting louder and louder as I spoke. Jere nodded and pointed at me as he chewed his sandwich. We asked him if he wanted to play, which he did. It was his first year here and he needed someone to hang out with. He was the main hero in many of our deadly stories.

"Yeah! We forgot it over the summer," Amber muttered as we were excused outside for recess. "we said that if we didn't remember, we owed each other a soda!" Amber whispered as we sat down at our picnic table. I was realizing that maybe; we could be the craziest people on earth, or that we could have something to do with Charles' "death".

"Are you saying that unless we're absolutely crazy, your 3rd grade game might connected to all of this?" Kennedy replied in a not so friendly tone. I knew that Kennedy loves a little mystery, adventure, and fun, but now anyone of us could be pulled to what we now like to call, the "Death Call".

As the day went on, all I thought about was the "Death Call", all the pieces that made sense and all the pieces that didn't. It was crazy to think that maybe, 4 years ago, we might've put this on ourselves. It made zero sense, but if I thought for a second, it kinda did. I was nervous and the uneasy feeling that the school's survival was in our hands for some reason. It was finally time to go home, and I was at the gym faster than ever.

"Alright everybody. You know the expectations. Let's get going so you guys can go home," Mr. Griffin said. The batches started going and everything seemed to go alright, for the moment. But about 25 minutes later, just like yesterday, one person was called instead of a whole batch. Barrett Dachelet, Amber's younger brother.

"No. No no no. This is not happening," Amber hissed. She dropped her backpack and started to confront Mr. Griffin.

"Stop! Barrett don't go out there. You can't make him!" Amber shouted. She tried to stand up, stopped by Jere, Kennedy and I as we tried to sit her back down. We almost lost our grip on her, when Mr. Griffin's sharp words stopped all of us dead, frozen.

"Miss Dachelet, your brother's name was called. That means that your brother walks to his car and you continue to follow the expectations. Now, do you want a detention or not?" Mr. Griffin ended with warning tone as he led Barrett to the door. Amber, Kennedy, Jere, and I raced to the door and kept the door open as we peered outside. We tried to yell and scream at Barrett but it was like he couldn't hear a thing, including us. He went on the swing and started swinging, just like Charles. After five minutes, Barrett was gone. Amber started crying as we slowly yet quickly sat back down with our stuff.

"Melissa Logan, to Mrs. Genie's office. Melissa Logan to Mrs. Genie's office. Thank you." The loudspeakers announced. I groaned as I stood up and walked towards my fate. I didn't know exactly what I was up against, but I knew one thing: Mrs. Genie was probably up to something and apparently; I'm in the way.

"Ms. Logan! Sit down, let's talk," Mrs. Genie requested as I pulled a chair out and sat in it, slumping to the side of the chair.

"Yes, Mrs. Genie? Am I in some short of trouble?" I inquired. She looked at me and gave me a stare that have only haunted me in some of my greatest fears.

"Oh Melissa! I just want to ask you a question and then you can go. Your father's looking for you anyway. I wanted to know if you knew anything about what has been happening in the gym during pick up these past few days," Mrs. Genie mentioned quietly. I almost laughed, standing up and looking this devil straight in the eye.

"I only know two things Mrs. Genie. One, I have no idea what's going on. Two, I think you're asking the wrong person. Ask yourself. You're in charge around here, so I think you should know. Have a nice afternoon Mrs. Genie." I said with a sweet smile as I proudly exited Mrs. Genie's office.

"You know Melissa, when I come down to the gym to get my kids and one of them isn't there, it upsets and worries me," my father said in the most doubtful way as I entered his classroom, the boys screaming behind him as they played tug of war with a hopeless jacket. I just shrugged, with being so stressed and tired, and fell onto his chair in the corner of the room.

"It is not my fault, dad! I was in the gym, sitting quietly and watching the brutal events in the gym, when Mrs. Genie called me over the loudspeaker to her office for a little chat. I was just doing what I was told," I sighed. My dad looked over at me suspiciously, but soon shook his head when seeing my stressful and upset face.

"What did she want? You aren't in trouble, are you?" my dad wondered as he started to pack his things together and get the boys under some sort of control. I stood up and gathered my stuff as well.

"I'm not in any trouble! Ms. Genie just wanted to ask me a question about the weird things going on during pickup. She acts like I have something to do with it," I replied, not forgetting to add a dramatic "sheesh" at the end. As we drove home, all I could think about was all the possible events that could happen next week.

Monday, March 12, 2018. Recess.

Today was even worst, which I thought wasn't possible. Apparently, they found Barrett's killer and there's a search party after him. I groaned, and it got louder after yet another realization that it is possible that Jere, Amber and I could've started all of this mess.

"Ok. Samira, Faye, I need your help. I need something to take my mind off of all this crazy business," I muttered as we walked over to our picnic bench and watch Jere, Travis, Trent, and Gavin play football on the field. All of a sudden, Amber grabbed me by the arm and whipped me around to face her.

"You are not taking your mind off this," Amber whispered with a warning tone in her voice, "I know that it didn't matter as much with Charles, but now my brother is gone. We need to do something!" Amber exclaimed at me. My anger immediately started to boil up, from Mrs. Genie, from this "Death Call", and I got so frustrated that I yanked her hand off of me and pushed her back. I pointed at her and locked my eyes with her eyes.

"Don't you realize that I just maybe don't know what to do? Don't you know that I have no freaking idea what is going on either and that I'm scared too?" my voice vibrating with fear, "I want to help and get your brother back, but we need a crew and a plan before we go after something that we don't even know anything about!" I ended with a shout as I marched off to a place to cool off.

Soon enough, I was overwhelmed with frustration and fear. I was scared and nervous and felt like everyone was waiting for me, just me, to do something. I shook in surprise when I heard soft footsteps walk towards me.

"Hey," Kennedy said as she sat down next to me. I breathed and continued to softly cry as I leaned onto Kennedy's shoulder. Kennedy never always knew what was wrong, but she was always there for me and for all of us.

"I'm scared Kennedy," I finally admitted in tears, "I feel like everyone is counting on me and I have know idea what we should do." All Kennedy did was hug me even tighter and told me it was going to be okay. We soon saw Amber, Samira, Faye, Belle, Lacey, Abree, and Lucy ambled over and they sat around me. I could almost immediately tell that we were all scared about this "Death Call".

"We all talked. We're going to solve this, whatever it is, together. We're going to stop the "Death Call"," Lucy said with some confidence in her voice. I slowly stood up, my worry drying up inside of me. Lucy was right. All of this needs to stop. The more we wait, the more kids that will be taken. We were the team that was going to find "Death Call", and make sure it stops calling.

The rest of the day gradually went by, including pick up. Today, Martin was taken. I guess I was ok at the moment, but all of my friends and I knew that I was holding back tears. My friends and I came to Belle's house later to discuss our plan, but only hopeful ideas tumbled out of our minds. We had no solid plan yet, but we all believe that something will turn up before we know it. As I went home, I kind of smiled. I will get our brothers back and Charles back. All of this will be gone before we know it.

TWO WEEKS LATER...

Monday, March 26, 2018.
5:40 in the evening after school.

"Melissa! This is going out of control! Half of an entire class is gone!" Amber hissed into her phone during a group phone chat.

"I know, I know. 14 kids, which includes my Gale, my Martin, Kennedy's brother Spencer, Barrett, Charles, and 9 others," I whispered, my head filling with dread. We believed that we would find something before we knew it, but instead we have 14 kids missing. 4 of them being our siblings.

"What do we do?" Belle asked nervously. I shrugged and dived into what looked like my square of misery instead of my bed.

"I don't know, but I do know that we need a plan and get our act together or half the school will be gone before we knew anything happened," Samira snapped. I groaned and before anyone could say anything, I quickly said that we could have a meeting tomorrow during school and hanged up. I sat up and was about to go get my brothers to play outside or watch TV, when I stopped. *My brothers are gone, and I haven't seen them for a week and a half,* I thought. I slammed my door in fury and fell back onto my square of misery.

THE DEATH CALL

After long 10 minutes of staring at my flavorless ceiling, I thought of something. I sprang up to my computer, typed up **The Death Call,** and jammed my finger on the search button. Thousands of answers came up unto the screen. I scrolled down until I came across a really weird site about mythical and mysterious events. I clicked on it and a paragraph came up about the "Death Call". The first 12 sentences convinced me that this can help us.

Have kids in your school been "leaving" and not coming back? Have you seen your fellow classmates kind of disappear out of nowhere? This is probably the "Death Call". If you are asking where it comes from, it's from little kids! Little kids play games like this all the time and say to their friends all the time that they will remember this game when they get older. The problem is that it is a little kid game, so the game "threatens" the kids to try to remember it by the time they're in 6th or 7th grade. If they don't, the game makes itself real and *puts itself as a curse over the school. If you are wondering how to stop it, there is only one way to do it. The kids that played the game and made the curse have to disappear the same way all the other kids did. All the kids are taken somewhere. There, they must convince the "Death Call" to free all the kids and they have to say that you loved the game when you played it. Hope that helps:)-RR*

I grinned as I printed out the page so I can show it to everyone and see what they think.

Tuesday, March 27, 2018.
7:30 in the morning.

"Hey! Wait up!" I screamed as I ran after my friend Abree and caught up to her at the school steps. She laughed as she pulled me in for a bear hug and we walked into the school building. I sat down at my homeroom seat and Amber, Faye, Jere and Samira immediately surrounded me.

"I heard that you found something to help us last night, Melissa," Faye implied as she sat down next to me. I nodded and beckoned for Amber, Faye, Samira, and Jere to lean in even closer so that Mr. Griffin wouldn't be able to hear us.

"Yes, I did. I searched the "Death Call" and found this weird mythical and mysterious site that told me how the "Death Call" came to be and how to stop it," I whispered as I pulled out the copy, took a breath, and continued, "it told me that little kids make the curse. They play it, say they will remember it, and then the game "threatens" the kids to remember the game by the time they're in 6th or 7th grade. If they don't, the game will become a curse over the school," I ended with a sigh. Everyone nodded carefully as they read the rest of the paper.

"It says that the kids that played the game/made the curse has to disappear the same way the other kids did and then they must convince the "Death Call" to free all the kids, saying that you loved the game when you played it," Samira acknowledged quietly as she passed the paper back to me.

"So, what's the plan?" Faye asked. I looked around and laughed when I saw that they haven't connected the dots yet.

"Isn't it obvious? Amber and I are going to disappear and go to the "Death Call"," I answered as I got my stuff and headed to Period 1.

I sat down and started to work on my project when Kennedy charged towards me and grabbed me by the arm.

"Melissa, you're insane. Are you actually thinking about doing this?" Kennedy hissed as she harshly pulled me aside from the class. I stared at her like *she* was insane and tugged her off of me.

"Kennedy, are you listening to yourself? Your brother is gone, both of mine are gone, Amber's brother is gone, and if we keep this up, almost 28 students will be gone. We have no other choice. We have to do this." I quickly hugged her and continued to work on my project until class was over. As I walked to basketball elective after L.A. class, I suddenly began to hear voices chat in my head. I yelled and dropped to my knees, the voices getting louder. I screamed and almost banged my head against the wall, the voices now even louder and hurting my head. It was only when some 8th graders escorted me to the nurse when I actually listened to the words.

I will come. I will come. I will come to your school. I will come. I will become a human creature. I will…

I was alert and in pain all day, crying as I ran home and ran into my room. I rushed to my computer and went to the same site as last time, scrolling past where I stopped reading before. I started to panic as I read it all over again and the realization finally reached my head.

Oh! By the way, if you wait too long to stop the "Death Call", the game will become a human form and do even more horrible things to your school. Before it does that though, it starts talking to the kids that made the curse. Be careful and hurry! -RR

By the time I got to the end of the page, I was panting and sobbing all over myself. It wasn't until 5 minutes later that I was able to even move, let alone get a snack and change into my pjs. The voices in my head finally stopped, but I knew for sure that they would come back eventually. I was still trying to breathe and control my shivering from crying as I grabbed my phone and called Amber. She answered on the first ring.

"Melissa? What's wrong? Are you trembling? Why are your teeth chattering? I can hear it all through the phone," Amber said nervously. I swallowed my terror and explained everything, from the voices to the human form of the game. Soon, I wasn't the only person trembling with chattering teeth.

"Wait, so you're saying that you are hearing the game's voice, in your head?!" Amber whispered yet shrieked through the phone. I nodded, and suddenly, I heard crying through the phone a few seconds later. I slowly stood up, holding my phone in both hands.

"Amber? Amber are you ok?" I begged frantically. All I heard was a mumbling sound. Words. It was Amber. Talking.

"Stop. Stop, make it stop!" Amber mumbled, which eventually turned into a scream. *She was hearing the game in her head as well,* I thought. Before I was even certain that that was the situation, Amber hanged up on me. I decided to not call her back; I knew she probably needed her space. The game's voice came back, and I groaned as I slowly sat in the middle of my room. After the voice finally went away, I started to cry and curled myself into a ball, rocking back and forth in horror at the words that were just repeatedly screamed at me.

In six days time, I will become a human and visit your school. You better watch out, because a lot more people will be taken/hurt.

Wednesday, March 28, 2018.
6:30 in the morning.

I woke up surrounded in blankets, stuffed animals, and a tray of cereal and yogurt. Apparently, my dad must've put me to bed and brought me breakfast. I tried to get out of bed, but suddenly felt really sick to my stomach. I groaned and fell back in my bed just as my dad came into the room. He sat down and looked at me with a happy yet concerning face.

"Hey sweetie. When I put you to bed, you had a terrible flu, and your stomach and head looked bad. You're staying home from school today, and by the looks of it, you'll probably be home for the rest of the week," My dad said with a sigh. I sighed as well; feeling relieved to be staying home, but decided to lie in bed crying instead of rejoicing.

"What's wrong, sugar pie?" My dad asked as he sat down next to me and I leaned into his shoulder. I shook my head and turned to face him.

"I'm just in a lot of pain, and I miss Martin and Gale. I miss them very much. I want them found and here with us," I said, continuing to cry in my dad's arms. He nodded and after a while, gradually walked out of the room. He came back with the usual "staying home alone" rules, kissed me on the forehead, and left for school. Just as I finished picking out a gray sweater, black pants, light brown snug boots, and pulling my hair up in a messy bun, I got a text from Jere.

Melissa,
Sorry that you're sick, I know being sick sucks. Anyway, you know how my fam and I are leaving for Georgia today to visit my cousins?

Come have a picnic with us before we leave.
Love ya! - Jere

I smiled and as I packed up a few things in my tote, answered him.

Jere,
I would love to! Will be at your house in a moment. - Melissa

I breathed as I slowly walked out the front door and with another short intake of breath, took a short walk over to Jere's house. I knocked on the door and out appeared Jere's little brother, Kade. His smile grew bigger and bigger the longer he looked at me, due to the fact that he adored me. When Jere and I would babysit Kade together, he would want me to tuck him in for bed at night instead of his own brother. He ran towards me and I laughed as I slowly bent down to hug him.

"Melissa! You came! How are you?" he exclaimed. I shrugged but smiled as Kade continued to embrace me. Just as I was standing back up, Travis, Jere's twin brother, came striding through the door.

"Hey Melissa! Glad you could make it!" Travis exclaimed, laughing once he saw Kade strangling my legs. After I said hi to his parents, Kaela and Caden, we were all set to go for a picnic and a trip to the airport, except for the fact that Jere wasn't outside with us.

"Where's Jere?" I asked. Jere's family suddenly started to burst out in laughter and started to usher me towards the front door.

"Jeremiah's dressed and ready to go, but is still in bed. He proclaimed that he will not get out of bed until his girl pulls him out," Kaela said while giggling. I started laughing too as Kade released me and pushed me into the house.

"Go get your beau, Melissa," Kade smirked. I laughed as I went inside and towards Jere and Travis's bedroom. Once I got there, I was on the verge of exploding with giggles.

Jere was fake snoring and was smothered with blankets on his messy bed. I walked over to him, grabbed a pillow from the ground and smacked him in the head with it.

"Jere, it's time to go," I exclaimed sternly. He moved around, but stayed buried in his cave of blankets. I silently giggled and smacked him again.

"Mom, I told you! I'm not leaving this bed until my precious is here to get me," Jere moaned as he slowly shook his head. I kept laughing in my sweater, almost falling over trying to regain myself. I finally stood up and lifted a blanket so that I could see his face.

"It's me, Melissa! Your girl! You didn't even hear me. I called you Jere, not Jeremiah," I commented softly. After a few moments, Jere opened one eye. He grinned and in 5 seconds, he sprang up from all of his blankets and tackled me. I screamed and hit him with a pillow yet again.

27

I finally pushed him back unto the bed, holding the end of the pillow to his throat while giggling.

"Melissa! It's you! You made it! I thought you were my mom!" Jere implied while I pulled him up and quickly kissed his cheek. I grabbed his hand and his suitcase and led both outside to everyone else. We gathered all of our stuff and took a quick walk to the park that's right near both of our houses.

"Ok, Melissa. You ready?" Jere suddenly asked as we arrived to the park sidewalk. I looked at him in confusion but nodded as Jere took my hand and led me into the park. We turned a final corner and I gasped at what I saw. Jere and his family set up a beautiful picnic near my favorite lake with flowers and a we'll miss you sign! I laughed and grinned as we walked over and plummeted into a lovely fuzzy picnic blanket. I had only eaten one strawberry before the three boys attacked me and I was (with multiple stops) running around the park, chasing them as they chased me. We played for a while longer and ate lunch together, and then it was finally time get in the van and drive up to the airport. After finishing the journey of parking and walking up to the entrance of the airport from the parking lot, I wrapped my arms around him and gave him a big hug.

"I'm gonna miss you, my Jere," I sighed. He wrapped his arms around me and held me close right back.

"I'll miss you too, my Melissa. But it will all be fine. It's only a few days, until Saturday I think. Remember the rules. No falling for other guys and have fun," Jere smiled. I laughed and smiled as well. He kissed me and after being scolded by his father, he let go and waved. I waved back and got into the nearest cab to take me home. After getting inside my house, I lied down and watched stuff on Netflix for a while, taking my mind off of anything and everything. Just after 4, Kennedy called and said that Faye was taken. A big double decker bus hit me with guilt and sadness at the fact that my friends were now being taken as well. Moments later, my dad walked in with a sincere smile, my homework, and my assignments. He asked me about my day and I shrugged, saying that I hanged out with Jere and his family before they left for Georgia, and then hung out at home. He smiled and after checking my still high temperature, left the room. I grabbed my stuff and my snack and started to work.

After finishing my grueling homework from Mr.Kennicott, I got a wonderful email from the one and only Mrs. Genie. I just groaned and read it while I started my math assignments and homework.

Dear Melissa Logan,
I'm sorry that you weren't able to attend school today or for the rest of the week. Frankly, you missed a lot. Your dear friend Faye, she left unexpected today and I honestly don't think she will be coming back. Anyway, I was wondering if you would want to start in basketball and be on the girls team for the season this year. There is

this new girl coming in five days who loves basketball and was wondering if you could be her shadow and connect with her more through basketball. Mrs. Eagle will be coach this year so you could email her about that. Thank you Melissa! See you in five days!

From your lovely principal,
Mrs. Genie

I was completely confused. I couldn't believe that she knew all of this about me. I absolutely love playing basketball, and I'm really good at it. I also love introducing people to new things and making new friends. It's a weird hobby, but I still love it. I emailed her back and lay back in my chair with relief and shock that Mrs.Genie is actually being _nice_, despite the lingering feeling that this is a trick or blackmail.

Dear Mrs.Genie,
Thanks for your email!?! I am devastated as well that I can't be at school for the rest of the week. I'm very worried about Faye as well. I love basketball, and I would love to help this new student be more comfortable at our school and bond with her over shooting hoops! I'll email Mrs.Eagle about joining the girls' team.

Thank you and see you in five days as well!

From your lovely student,
Melissa Logan

Regardless of my suspicions of the email and my overwhelming hate for Ms. Genie, I was actually pretty excited about this new student and being in basketball. But as I went to sleep later that night, all I could think about was that the "new student" could be the game's human form. I didn't want to be friends with my own evil creation, but what if she isn't the game's human form? I would be rejecting and avoiding a possible friend, a possible new crew member. Right before I shut my eyes, my computer dinged. I rolled out of bed and went to my email. It was Mrs. Genie yet again.

Dear Melissa Logan,
By the way, the new girl's name is Rosemary Raven and her email is rosemaryraven7@gmail.com in case you wanted or needed it. Good night.

From your lovely principal,
Mrs. Genie

I slowly crept back in bed and shivered as I thought about the girl's name. Rosemary Raven. That sounds like a name of a person that I would not like to be friends with. So is Rosemary the game's human form? But the girl's initials are RR, which are the initials of the person who wrote that page on the "Death Call", so that means she isn't bad, right? I had so many thoughts that I couldn't think, but I knew one thing. Whether she was my enemy or not, I was going to have an interesting day when I return to school.

Thursday, March 29, 2018.
2:29 in the afternoon.

The next day was so and so. I watched Netflix and danced when I didn't hear "The Voice" or feel like throwing up. At around 2:30, I was dancing to a song when I heard three loud knocks on the front door. I stopped dancing, paused the music, and immediately went through my "people-who-would-knock-at-my-door" list. Martin and Gale, gone. Dad, at school. Any of my friends, at school. The mailman, its Thursday, not Monday. Neighbors, all at work or school. I put down my phone and slowly walked to the door. I peered through the door hole and couldn't see anyone there. After a few moments, I shrugged and started to walk away, when the door was banged on again.

"Come on, Melissa. You're not like a cat, who went to the best place in the world and didn't have fun. I least there were some good times with you," I hear a young voice call through the door. I stopped dead in my tracks and froze all around, including the tear on my cheek. That was the phrase (or "The Reason" is what I call it) that my mom told me whenever I had bad days when she was **actually around.** I turned around, opened the door, and I gasped. My mother; Teresa. I haven't seen my mom in almost a year and a half, yet there she was. I wanted to run to her, hug her and tell her all about what has happened since she was last here, but all I felt was hatred and pain for her just ditching us out of nowhere and never being there for my dad, Martin, Gale, and I. I almost slammed the door in her face when she stuck her hand out and stopped the door and myself.

"Melissa, please. Can we talk? I heard that you were sick and assumed you were here so-," Teresa begged as I tried my hardest to shut the door. I swung open the door again and glared at her with all my hatred that I had stored in me, which was a ton.

"What do you want?" I snarled as I gripped the door, prepared to fully slam the door right in her face if an inch of me is annoyed. She started to walk towards me, but I whipped my hand in front of me.

"Don't touch me, come near me, or even take another step," I exclaimed with anger, "I asked you a question, and now you need to answer it. What do you want and why are you here?" I ended with a snarl. She had a shocked expression on her face, but didn't seem surprised either.

"I came to talk to you. If you don't want to talk to me, then you can just listen. If you don't want to do that either, then I'll leave. Can I come in? Please?" she asked. I could tell she really wanted to, and I honestly wanted to talk to her too, about a lot of things. But I'm just not ready yet.

"Can you give me a minute? Then, maybe, I'll let you in so we can talk. Stay there," I replied with a sort of calm tone. She nodded and I gently shut the door, I turned around and rushed to my room.

Ok Melissa. You have been waiting for this moment for a long time but never thought it would happen. What should I do? I thought as I nervously sat on my bed. *I want to talk to her, but I'm not ready. Should talk to her tomorrow? Is that enough time to be prepared and ready for this?*

I breathed in and out, ran back downstairs and opened the door.

"Teresa? I am just not ready for this right now. I need a little more time and then we can talk. What about you coming over tomorrow? I'm staying home tomorrow too so," I explained slowly. My mom kind of grinned and started to back out of the porch.

"Thanks for telling me. I totally understand. See you then?" My mom suggested. I nodded and started to close the door.

"Bye, Teresa," I smiled as I closed the door. She waved and walked towards her car. I quickly grabbed an apple and watched her drive away. It was only then that I decided to breath. I ran upstairs and stared at my blank computer screen, realizing that it would be 4 soon. I started up my computer and skyped all of my friends at exactly 4:10, and they all popped up on the first ring. I was so excited to tell them about Teresa. They all loved her as well and were as devastated as my family was when she left.

"Hey Melissa! How's life?" Belle asked as I got my notepad for any important details.

"I'm fine. You guys have no idea what happened just a few minutes ago! But first, how was school?" I implied sternly. All of my friends suddenly had mixed expressions after that, so I got prepared for the worst.

"Well, the news say that Faye ran away and no one can find her," Samira started," her parents are really worried about her," I shrugged and spinned around in my chair. I missed her really badly and this is really just getting out of control.

"So, Spanish was… Spanish. L.A we worked on our big discussions next week. Math we just did group activities and just practiced. Lunch and Recess was as usual. Social Studies was just a boring class about WWII. Science was just notes, notes, notes!!" Kennedy said with laughs and bored expressions, but she didn't say anything about if there were any fiascos during pick up.

"Well? Were there any fiascos?" I asked, gripping my desk surface at their concerned faces.

"Well, Peter from 6th was taken today," Amber sighed, looking like she was disappointed, yet not on the caring side of the situation. I knew there was more, but Amber didn't look ready to say anything more. It took a few silent minutes before Amber finally spoke up.

"Ok, here's what else happened. Luckily, it happened during Social Studies so I didn't miss anything important or whatever. Anyway, I started hearing The Voice, but what it said was really concerning to me and scary," Amber said, waiting for everyone to take it in. As far as everyone has been told, The Voice is really scary and gives you clues.

"So, what did it say?" Lucy said impatiently, gripping the edges of her computer, making her hands look ghost pale. Amber took a deep breath and began saying what I assume to be exactly what The Voice said to her.

"It said, *'Amber, do you really think you can solve this problem? You and your wonderful friend Melissa are just weak and unable to save your school. I almost feel bad for you. You and Melissa are getting closer and closer to finding out some shocking truths and will also come close to possibly losing people you love. Don't blame me if in the next few days you guys get hurt. Blame yourselves.'* and after that it was just mumbling gibberish at me until Social Studies ended." Amber ended softly as she tried her hardest to stop shivering. I quickly regained myself and looked at them with a straight face as I began my own day's story.

"My day was fine, I guess. But nothing could prepare me for what was coming at around 2:30 precisely," I said as everyone leaned in, "someone knocked on the door, so I looked through the door hole and nobody was there. I started to walk away when I heard someone say "The Reason" through the door. I turned around, opened the door, and there stood Teresa," I ended dramatically as I lay on my bed with my computer to listen to all the comments.

"WHAT!?!" The girls screamed. They literally asked a million times if I was joking and just to prove them wrong, I showed them a picture of her at the door from our family's security camera. They couldn't believe it and wanted to know all about how I reacted.

"Well, I first I glared at her and asked her what she wanted and why she was here in a snarling voice. I even tried to slam the door at her. She asked if we could talk, and after a minute of consideration, I said yes but not today, I'm not ready. So I said we would talk tomorrow. So yeah," I ended, not even knowing an hour and a half later how I felt about it all. They couldn't believe that I didn't just let her in to talk and that I didn't embrace her, but they don't get it. After 1 ½ years of her not being there for us, it's super hard to just let her back in. I need time before I jump into uncertainty. Anyway, we talked for another 10 minutes and then we hanged up. 5 minutes later I finally got back out of bed, but felt horrible for some reason. Luckily my dad came home minutes later and I called to him and asked him to get me a snack. He came in with a popcorn snack with water, my homework, and missing assignments. He then plunged into the now interesting question of how my day was.

"It was good and very relaxed, and actually Teresa came for a visit," I said, waiting for dad to scream or be really upset, but he wasn't. We just snuggled together, multiple sighs shared between the two of us. He softly kissed my forehead and

with a final sigh, left the room. I was surprised by
his reaction, but understood. My dad is one of the
calmest people I know.

After finishing my Math and L.A
assignments and homework, I heard a ding on my
computer. I rushed over to see if Mrs. Genie
emailed again, but instead it was Amber.

Melissa,
Something is going to happen that's really bad,
and it's going to happen soon. There was a letter
for me that I saw after school today, and
Rosemary Raven signed it? I have no idea who
she is but she knows something about the
"Death Call". Look at what it said:

Dear Amber Dachelet,
Hello! My name is Rosemary. Rosemary
Raven. I hear that you're dealing with what
you call the "Death Call"? Well, it's about
to get a lot worse. You and Melissa better
prepare for an unexpected visit at 5:00
tonight precisely. Good Luck!

So yeah, that's super creepy. Good luck,
I guess?

From,
Amber

I was totally creeped out! Now I know that Rosemary _was_ the human form of the game, right? Does that mean that if Rosemary Raven wrote the page on that weird site, is it all a joke? That's not how to make this all go away? But what's the deal if she didn't write it, is she good or bad? I had no idea what any of this means, but I need to figure it out quickly, because it's 4:30. I hastened to finish up the rest of my homework, make a 5-minute plan, email Amber back and then email Rosemary Raven.

Amber,
Don't panic. Everything will be ok. Meet me at the park at in the lab in 15 minutes. I have everything under control. Just trust me, ok?
Meet you in a few.

From,
Melissa

Ok, that was easy. Next will be emailing Rosemary. I don't even know what to say to her, I don't even know which side she's on! But I cracked my knuckles anyway to try and be tough and wrote away.

Rosemary Raven,
Hello pipsqueak, it's Melissa here. I hear the horror will come at 5:00 huh? Well, if you actually want to "bring the horror", then act like a man. Meet Amber and I at the park in 16 minutes. See you there.

From,
Melissa Logan

Although I felt more confident after the send button was pushed, I knew that I had to get to Amber and see Rosemary before I can really take her. I quickly pulled on a sweater and jeans, braided my hair and grabbed my karate stick, just in case. I grabbed my phone and slowly yet rapidly ran downstairs, my upset stomach tumbling all the way down. As I grabbed an apple and started to go outside to get my bicycle, I heard my dad call me back into the house and into his office.

"Yes, dad? Is there a problem? I finished my homework if you wanted to know," I said as I moved towards the door. He shook his head and waved me over to him.

"Where are you going? To the park I'm guessing?" he implied as I came and sat down next to him. I nodded and kissed him on the cheek. He nodded as well and sat up in his chair.

"I don't know, you're sick. I guess, as long as someone is with you and you are back by 7:00, you can go," He sighed as I smiled and swiftly hugged him. I rushed outside and unto my bike; only having 6 minutes left. I sped to the park and ran the rest of the way to the lab, where Amber was waiting for me.

"Melissa, I'm really nervous. What is going to happen? Why are we even here?" Amber asked as she paced back and forth between our two trees. I shrugged and groaned as I sat down on my rock.

"It's going to be alright, Amber. I just wanted to get Rosemary Raven and ourselves out of our houses so that she can't hurt our parents. Rosemary is this new girl coming to school on Monday. I think that she is the human form of the game, but I'm not sure," I sighed. Amber nodded and we started to breathe more calmly as we watched the river near our lab flow through the twigs and rocks.

Suddenly, a strong invisible force pushed us off the rocks, over a small bush and sent us rolling down the hill. I screamed as I landed on the ground, my back enlightening with pain and my lungs out of breath. I gradually jumped up, pulled Amber up with me, and looked around. There was no one at the park, no wind, and everything was very quiet.

"Melissa? What is that surrounding us?" Amber whispered, as if getting any louder would cause a commotion. I shook my head and we huddled even closer together. A thick purple circle of what looked like fog started to form around us and another strong invisible force threw us to the ground. Pain engulfed me yet again as I saw through my now swollen eyes that the fog had turned into a young girl.

"Wow. You guys are smart for being wimps. I was surprised how quickly miss Melissa here found out that I was the human form of the game. I mean, really, I'm impressed. Anyway, ready for the horror, Melissa?" Rosemary snarled as a third invisible force gathered around us, "picked us up", and threw us towards a wall of sharp rocks. Seeing the rocks, I quickly wrapped my arms tightly around Amber and when getting to the wall, pushed my feet as hard as I could against it. We ricocheted off the wall and rammed into Rosemary, all three of us falling in a heap on the ground. I got up as quick as I could and pounced on Rosemary.

Wow. She sure does look pretty for being such a creep, I thought as I grabbed her by the arms, pinning her against the grass and gave her the best snarling face that a person can give someone else.

"If you really want to give us horror, I'll just return the favor by giving you some first," I snapped at her while she struggled to break free. Suddenly, she smiled at me and started laughing at me. I looked at her with confusion and she gave me a straight face.

"I would really like you to, Melissa, but I think I'm honestly too cool for you to *horrify* me," she explained with dramatic gestures. A second later, she disappeared from under me and I fell face first into the grass. Wondering how she could've possibly disappeared, I felt something under my leg. I dug from under my leg and grabbed a small device with buttons on it. I took one more glance and in seconds, I realized that this was probably how she disappeared and/or turned invisible. I heard someone coming up behind me and without a second to lose or a moment to think, I pressed a button, stood up, and sprinted away from where I was. I turned around and saw Rosemary rush right by where I used to be and stopped in total confusion. I grinned with sheer pleasure and thought of an idea.

I ran to Amber and pulled her deep into the lab, pressing the button to reappear and smiled at her. She grinned at me back, but I knew she was shaking with fear. I told her our new plan and we raced to edges of the grass area of the playground. Rosemary saw both of us and started running towards me, and Amber started to chase Rosemary. Once Rosemary was about 5 feet away from me, Amber was 10 feet away from me and was slowly gaining on Rosemary. Rosemary was about to snatch the front of my sweater when she tripped over a silver wire (that Kade, Trent, and I placed yesterday from our game), which gave Amber enough time to pounce on top of her. I turned invisible and ran to this huge rock that was right near the fallen bodies of Amber and Rosemary. I climbed all the way to the top of the sloped rock, so that if I fell off the rock, I would land right over where Amber and Rosemary happened to be. I waited until Amber had a free hand held out and I tossed the remote to her. She caught it tightly with one hand, while her other hand was busy strangling Rosemary. Finally, Rosemary got a hold of Amber and twisted her to the ground. Amber quickly disappeared from under Rosemary, and I knew that that was my cue.

Once Amber was back and safe near the lab, I jumped off of the huge rock, plummeting fast towards Rosemary. Seconds before I hit the ground, I grabbed Rosemary's jacket and pushed her down into the ground with me, Rosemary screaming as pain exploded throughout her back and her lungs shrieking for breath. Not too long later, Rosemary was on top of me, splattering my face with blood from her nose. I grinned and kicked her hard in her side. She groaned and as she was about to punch me, an invisible force (Amber) pulled Rosemary off of me and threw her towards the rock wall. Her body slammed into the rock and Rosemary slowly stood up, grinning with her multiple red polka (blood) dots. After Amber reappeared, Amber gave me the remote and I turned invisible. Rosemary started to run and collided Amber as they fell to the ground, punching and kicking each other. I ran back to our lab to quickly grab stash of rope. I ran back towards them when I stop dead in my tracks at the scene before me.

"Your last words are going to be screaming and begging for mercy, pipsqueak," Rosemary spat at Amber as she grabbed Amber by the neck and lifted her into the air. I stiffened as my fists were suddenly clenched around the rope and my anger started to boil up. *This ends now. Amber, you better get ready.* I thought. Amber and I found each other's eyes for a moment and winked. It's time.

I started running as fast as I could towards Rosemary. I jumped as high as I could into the air and kicked as hard as I could against Rosemary's back. She screamed and fell on her stomach as she released Amber's neck. Amber coughed abruptly as she leaned forward and helped me tie Rosemary's hands and feet with rope. I walked over to Rosemary as she lay on the now bloody ground and looked her straight in the eye, just like Ms. Genie.

"Did you like your horror, Rosemary? Oh, and I really think this remote would love the experience of fresh water," I ended by spitting in her face. I punched Rosemary right in the nose, threw the remote in the nearby river, and Amber and I started running towards our bikes. We rode back home and ran inside our houses. I clasped in my bed and instantly fell asleep, the feeling of only a temporary victory.

Friday, March 30, 2018.
7:45 in the morning.

I woke up the next morning feeling awful. I switched my head position and gently lifted my arms. I felt around me and realized that I had a cut lip, a bruised side and a bump on my head. I finally fluttered my eyes and saw Teresa sitting on the edge of my bed, looking very concerned. I screamed once my voice got to my mouth and hit her in the face with my pillow.

"What the heck are you doing in my room? On my bed? Get out and let me have my space, please!" I yelled, as I got ready to actually smack her. She quickly stood up and left the room, closing

45

the door behind her. I shook with fury and confusion as I pulled on a gray and white shirt with jeans, and looked out my window to see that my dad already left. As I grabbed my phone, I noticed a note on my notebook.

Dear Melissa,
Have a great day, okay? Teresa will be here when you wake up because she wants to talk to you. Please listen, alright? I know it's hard after all that's happened, but give your mom a second chance. I love you!

Be my young, strong girl. For me.
Love,
Dad

I sighed deeply as I finished getting ready and opened the door. I gradually walked down the stairs and peered pass the wall to see Teresa sitting awkwardly in the living room. I chuckled as I went to the kitchen and grabbed two glasses of oj and some chocolate donuts. I calmly walked into the living room, gave her a glass and a donut, and sat down. After a moment of caution, Teresa sat up and started to speak.

"I'm sorry about being in your room-" Teresa started rapidly, but quickly stopped when I lifted my hand.

"It's ok, Teresa. I'm sorry that I freaked out and hit you with a pillow. You technically have a right to be in my room. You and dad are not divorced, so this is you and dad's house, even though you have another house right now," I breathed, relieved that that part was over, "so, what did you want to talk about?" I gestured to her as I started to relax in my chair.

"I just wanted to say hi and hang out with you sweetie. And I had an idea for us and wanted to touch base with you first to see what you think about it," Teresa explained.

"Ok. So what's your new idea? I want to talk to you too," I replied, my mouth slowly starting to form into a smile.

"I was wondering if I could come back and live with you guys, be part of the family again. I made a horrible mistake when I left you, Martin, Gale, and your dad. I love all of you and want to be your mom again. Is that ok, with you?" Teresa asked slowly, like she was preparing for a scream or a yell, but all I did was sigh. *I want her to come back, to have my mom back, but I don't trust her. Not yet,* I thought.

"Can you give me a second to think about it?" I finally muttered, and without a yes or another word from either of us, I left the room and went into the dining room. I grabbed a chair and thought for a second about this really hard decision. But before I even made up my mind, I heard talking back in the living room. I stood up and peeked through the door of the dining room and saw Teresa talking intently on her phone.

"Please calm down, will agree with this. Melissa is a kind and thoughtful girl. She would give anyone a second chance if she believed they deserve it, and I deserve it, I assure you. I'll move in, kidnap Marvin and Gale and we're out of here... The girl and the father we can leave, we need Marvin and Gale," Teresa hissed through her phone. I couldn't believe it. My mom was using me? My father also, whom she loved, or used to I guess. Kidnap my brothers? I don't care what she plans to do with them; she's not getting them. She's not using my father and I, and she is *definitely* not moving back into this house. Once I heard Teresa get off the phone, I held back tears as I grabbed my phone and the living room security camera and stepped into the living room.

"Get out. Get out of this house, **my** house, right now Teresa," I snapped at her as she came towards me. I backed up and held out the hand with my phone. Teresa backed up as well and put her hands on her hips, her lips pursed.

"What do you mean sweetheart? You haven't even told me your answer about my idea. You like it, right?" Teresa replied sweetly, showing the first signs of worry. I smirked at her with disgust and sat down, my hand still out. I pressed play on the recording and showed her the footage while I spoke.

"Don't call me sweetheart Teresa. You are not stepping into my house ever again, so enjoy the view now. I heard your little chat on the phone. You want to use my father and I to kidnap my brothers? You might be their mom but they are not leaving this house with you after what you've done to us. You loved us, what happened? You know what? I don't even care. You have 5 minutes to get out of my house before I call the police," I snapped at her while she finished watching the tape. She looked at me in pure shock as she glued her feet to the ground and I tightened my fists around the camera. All the anger and sadness that I used to feel for her boiled up inside. I dropped the camera on the couch and smacked my mom in the face.

"GET OUT!!!!!!!" I screamed in her face, tears all over me. She still didn't move. I pushed her all the way to the door and threw her purse and half eaten donut on the porch. I slammed the door in her face and locked the door.

After meeting and talking with the police and crying for an hour, I finally breathed a little and rested my body on the couch. *I wonder who she was talking to*, my troubled mind thought. I suddenly got so angry with all of this that I went to the back porch and broke some of our garden pottery against the side of the garage. Suddenly, I heard the garage open. Dad was home.

He ran up to me and asked my how my day was, but all I did was cry. I fell into his arms and gave him what was in my hand. One of the pottery pots that I broke as a pot Teresa and I made when I was little. The piece that I was holding was where Teresa wrote in purple paint, "I will always love you and be there for you." He sighed, carried me inside and I told him what happened. At first he didn't believe me so I showed him the footage from the living room and the dining room. My dad and I then cried for a while after that. My dad asked me if I wanted to throw away the pot. I said yes but not the piece that I had in my hand. That piece is still a part of me, in one way or another. Dad gave me a huge hug, saying that I was brave.

We ate out and after homework I cried myself to sleep for two reasons:

1. Teresa took my trust and my heart for her and crushed it all

2. It was the second time that I have ever seen my dad cry

FIRST DAY BACK AT SCHOOL...

Monday, April 2, 2018.
6:05 in the morning.

I woke up feeling drowsy and pain was all over me. I got ready with no music and no sympathy, still sickened by Friday's events. Packing my backpack for the day, I heard my phone ringing for the fifth time that morning. It was Teresa. Is she an idiot, thinking that I would <u>actually</u> answer her? Plus, after someone has tried calling someone five times, you'd think that they would stop trying, right? I jammed my finger unto the hang up button and threw my phone in my backpack as I trudged downstairs to see a warm breakfast and my dad. I gave him a hug, quickly ate my breakfast, and left the house. Kennedy was waiting for me outside with open arms, the first one to hear the horrible news. I ran into her arms and we embraced each other as we walked to school.

"Are you sure you don't want to tell anyone else about this? Only having Samira, Lucy and myself know is a small circle of support if you have to deal with school all day-" Kennedy said right before we entered the school building. I gave her a reassuring look and we entered the building hoping for the very best.

As I walked into the building, I totally regretted ever going to school. There she was. Miss Rosemary Raven. I knew that I was in for it after our fight two days ago, but grinned at the thought that Amber and I won, we beat her. I walked past her, nudging her in the shoulder as I passed and beckoned her to come with me for the school tour. Throughout the beginning of the day, we both kept ourselves at the neutral stage, with friendly nods and short but pleasant conversations. There were some ugly glances at times I admit, but at other times it was just fine. But there was one thing that I couldn't get off my mind. In every class, she sat next to me, in front of me, or behind me. I know Mrs. Genie said that I would be her guide and all, but I don't need to deal with this creep being **this** close to me every moment of the day. After the brief tour and explanation of the lunch and recess procedure, I raced away from Rosemary and out to the playground to meet up with my friends.

"So, how was this Rosemary?" Belle commented as I sat down to rest in the grass next to the gate, "Bruce's cage". I looked at all of them and shrugged.

"Well, she is still her pretty and frightening self, but she wasn't that bad. I had to sit in front of her, behind her, or next to her in every class though! We gave each other hard glares, but she was on the low side," I explained, trying not to make a big deal over it all. They all looked relieved that it wasn't that bad, but still looked concerned.

"It's going to get worse, I just know it. After how determined she was at the park? I know that she is steaming mad after we beat her," Amber said nervously. I was about to agree when Amber got forced to the ground. Rosemary was on her in second, her dark brown curls dripping over Amber's bruised face as more and more punches reached her. I rammed into Rosemary, knocking her over. Apparently, Rosemary regained power and strength as she automatically threw me off of her and I spiraled down the smooth hill. For a moment, I witnessed my friends huddled near a tree, watching us in pure horror. I tried reached out to them when I was pulled backwards towards Rosemary.

Rosemary grabbed my arms and dragged me to the top of either the swings or the slide. She shoved me off the equipment and I screamed as I crashed against the wood chips. A few seconds of unbearable pain went by until Rosemary was on top of me once again. She clutched my leg and stared at me with the meanest glare and the most enticing desire.

"This is going to hurt really bad, but _it is_ your turn for the horror," Rosemary hissed at me. I was about to punch her and kick her, when I heard something snap. I screamed at the pain that bolted through my left leg as I kicked Rosemary in the face with my usable foot. I yelled for Faye and through clenched teeth I hissed with pain that I needed a teacher, and I needed one real soon...

1½ HOURS LATER....

I felt pain. That's all I felt. No anger, no sadness, no happiness, just dreadful pain. I opened one eye and saw my troubled dad and peaceful Amber. I opened my other eye and saw Teresa, her face pale and lips slightly parted as she stared at me. Once I found my voice, I demanded that she was out of this room and out of this hospital. After she left, I asked Amber and my dad what happened.

"Well, you know about the fight. After you told Faye to get the teacher, you passed out. I passed out as well. Belle went to get the teacher while Kennedy kept you and me company and Samira kept Rosemary from attacking again. When Ms. Genie, your dad, and the nurse came, Lucy told them what happened and then Mrs. Genie took Rosemary away and the nurse called the ambulance. Next thing we knew, your dad, you, and I were in the ambulance on the way to the hospital," Amber explained slowly as she held my hand tightly in mine. I just then realized that Amber was in a hospital bed as well. She had a broken arm, a bruised head and her other arm was bruised. I looked over to my dad and all he did was smile and relaxed in his chair next to me.

After another 2 hours, Amber and I finally got out of the hospital with casts, crutches, a wheelchair, and medicine. There was an email when I got back saying that Amber, Rosemary, and I were suspended for the rest of the week, even though Rosemary started the fight and we were hurt. I just got back to school, but was so relieved for another break. After finishing homework and finally going to bed, I was frustrated, concerned, and just had all of these feelings that I couldn't comprehend. But I knew that Rosemary is going to pay hard for what she did to us.

Saturday, April 7, 2018.
9:30 in the morning.

After 4 days of rest and learning how to work my crutches and my wheelchair, I felt great! After I had my breakfast with my new medicine and gradually pulled on a light purple sweater, dark jeans, knowing exactly what I wanted to do to start off my day. I wanted to get back at Rosemary, hard. I knew I needed a backup, a crew for this mission. In 10 minutes, I decided on Kennedy, Samira, Belle, and Amber. I called them up and they were here in my house in less than 15 minutes.

"What is this about, Melissa?" Belle complained as they walked into the living room. They lazily gathered around me as I pulled up the school's website.

"Well, I would like to first point out that Rosemary didn't get into any other trouble for attacking us and breaking our bones. All she had to do was not go to school for the rest of the week and write an apology letter to me and Amber," I muttered as I pulled out two letters that I got in the mail today and gave Amber her card. We opened our cards and there was a little piece of paper that said, "sorry I hurt you, Rosemary ✿" with a piece of bubble gum. I slammed the card into the trash, but kept the gum.

"Ok guys, let's cut to the chase. Rosemary needs to pay, badly. We need a plan to get back at her, and maybe even get some info from her. I chose you guys specifically because I know you will be great at this. Are you with me?" I asked them, smacking my gum against my tongue as I pulled out my rough draft of the plan. Gradually, each of them nodded. I nodded with them and started to show them my plan.

"Ok. Amber, you need to find out Rosemary's address on the school's website. Kennedy, you are in charge of the emails and emailing people. Belle, you need to make six average sized boxes with tops. Samira, I need 6 awesome paintball guns with a lot of paintballs. I am in charge of setting everything up. Let's get work!" I inquired. We started to get out computers, supplies, and got to work. For the next two hours, we worked on our jobs while listening to music. Teresa called 6 times throughout those 2 hours and I hanged up every single time, almost considering deleting her contact.

Apparently, Rosemary's house is right near all of our houses, at the end of a street two streets down from us. Belle made spectacular boxes that were perfect for our plan, and Samira's paintball guns were outstanding. I had set everything up, and Kennedy's email was perfection.

Rosemary,

Hello! This is Kennedy Lunt here. I'm pretty sure that you got a package from me a few minutes ago? Great. Take that to the park and maybe shoot some trees.

From,
Kennedy L.

"Can you please tell us the plan now?" Samira protested. I told her to hang on for one minute. After everything was set in the living room, I explained the final plan.

"Here is what we're going to do. After we put the paintball guns in the boxes, one of us is going to take one of the boxes to Rosemary's house, ring the doorbell and run. Then Kennedy will send the email she wrote. After that, we will take the rest of the boxes and go to the park. I will explain more there. Belle, do you mind delivering Rosemary's box? I would but wheelchairs are not the best for running away," I asked. Belle nodded and we started getting ready while Belle delivered the box.

A few minutes later, Belle was running back to our house, pumping her arms in front of her as she zoomed unto my porch. Once Belle got inside, Kennedy quickly pressed the send button for the email. We grabbed the boxes, Samira grabbing my wheelchair as I carried my box, and we ran or rolled as fast as we could to the park. We set the boxes around the edges of the field and ran or rolled to the huge rocks that surrounded the area.

"Here's the rest of the plan. When Rosemary gets here, she will shoot the paintball gun at a tree, like we told her to. That will trigger the cause and effect trap that I built yesterday with my dad. Once that is set, we will grab the paintball guns, run back to our rocks and start shooting her. At some point, she will fall into one of my other traps and we got her. Ready?" I asked, nervously smiling at all of them. They grinned back and ran to their spots. I slowly rolled back up to my rock with the help of Kennedy and grinned as some middle schoolers I invited from school and others came to the park to watch.

When a few minutes have passed by, Rosemary walked into the park, totally ignoring the school and public audience and also was completely unaware that Amber, Samira, Kennedy, Belle, and I were there, watching her. Rosemary pulled out her paintball gun and aimed it at the tree right near Samira. She shot it and and once the ball hit the tree, alarms started to ring. Rosemary dropped her gun and cautiously backed up into the middle of the field only to be more shocked. She watched the five of us grabbing something and running to the top of our rocks, and got especially annoyed when she saw Kennedy grab the last paintball gun and throw it up to me.

"FIRE!!" I roared. All of us started firing the paint balls at Rosemary. She was being destroyed by yellow, blue, red, and white splatters that hit her hard in the chest, face, arms, and legs. Although she looked desperate to run away, she just stood

there, frozen, as the paintballs kept
bombarding her.

Suddenly, all the paintballs stopped. Rosemary
looked up and saw me, ready to fire. She looked at
me the same way I looked her at the playground.
Why are you doing this? Why?? I had a split-
second decision to make. Should I shoot? I knew
that if I did shoot, she would be trapped. If I didn't
shoot, she would be safe. I didn't want to, but
besides, *she deserves it. Right?* I thought. I aimed
my gun right at her stomach, looked at her one
more time and fired the bright red ball. The ball
banged against her stomach, the red bursting all
around her. She wailed and fell backwards onto the
ground, a rectangular-shaped area opened up
under her and she fell into a black box. Finally, the
flaps on the sides of the box closed over her and
formed to lock her in.

Everyone cheered, pumping their fists in the
air, and in less than 10 minutes, everyone was
gone except for me, Samira, Amber, Kennedy, and
Belle. With my signal, we went to the box and
slowly carried it back to my backyard, placed it on
the ground, and carefully sat around the box.

"What do we do now? We can't just let her
out of the box, she'll either destroy us or run away,"
Belle breathed as we inched towards the box. I put
my hands on the box and pointed at the crack
between the two flaps of the box.

"I designed the box so that there are straps
with a lock, so when Rosemary fell in, the straps
tied her to the box and locked the straps. So when I
open the box, she's not going anywhere or doing

anything," I assured my crew as I began to unlock the locks on the box. After unlocking the last lock, I slowly opened all four flaps on the sides of the box.

We sprinted or rolled to the edges of the gates trapping us in the backyard, only to be terrified of what's in the box. There lay Rosemary, strapped to the bone with thick black rope and was covered with every color paintball you could think of. With one motion, we quickly went inside the house to think. As I closed the screen door, all I could see was Rosemary's eyes stare right into mine, boring into my skin.

Amber broke the silence first. "Well? What do we do with her?" she blurted out. They all looked at me and I shrugged. I had a plan, but now I'm not so sure. I grabbed my plan book and opened it to the last step, pushing it to the middle of the coffee table to let everyone read it in astonishment. They looked up at me with confused faces, pleading me to tell them the plan.

"My original plan was threaten her to tell us anything about the "Death Call". But know I'm not sure if we should do it," I mumbled, fingering with my necklace that my dad gave me the night that Teresa left.

"Well then, let's just let her go. I bet you anything that she'll just run back to her house after what we did to her," Kennedy replied. Knowing that it was our best plan at the moment, we walked back outside only to be shocked yet again. The body box was empty.

All we saw was that the inside of the box was covered with paintball splatters, the locks battered and covered with paint, and purple and green footsteps going out of my backyard and back towards her house. Once the stunning effect wore off, we noticed a note hanging off the side of the box. I read it and turned around, doubling over and starting to tear up. The others quickly read the note and urged me to tell them what was wrong, not understanding the different reactions from the note. I just nodded towards the note.

"You guys didn't is because you didn't read the whole note. You didn't read the part that was covered in blue paint," I muttered. They looked and read the entire note again, gasping and tears welling up in their eyes when finishing.

Very funny girls. I hope you're happy. I can't wait to destroy your lives on Monday! By the way, if you save everyone, don't blame me or anyone else if one of you aren't there to see it, if you know what I mean.

Rosemary

Even though it was only 5:30, I ate dinner early, said goodnight to my dad, and went straight to bed. I was so scared about Monday, and about the note. I know what she meant. She meant that if we saved the school, that one of the people in the school won't be around, or alive, <u>possibly</u>. Right before I was about to shut my eyes, my phone dinged. I looked at it and smiled, seeing that it was a text from my Jere.

Melissa,
Every time I look at the keyboard, I see that U and I are always together. Guess who's back in town? Do you want to meet me and hang out at the park?

Jere

I giggle. I love my Jere. He's so sweet. My giggle paused for a moment realizing that since he left for Georgia before I came back to school, he has not seen the horrors of Rosemary. He hasn't seen the damage that has happened to me. I slowly sit up and text him back as I turn my light back on.

Dear Jere,
I just wanted to tell you: You mean the world to me. You are the most amazing guy. You are sweet, kind, caring. I would be lost without you. I will never let you go.

Love,
Your girlfriend

P.S. I would love to go to the park and hang out. You have to pick me up though. ☺

I press send and slowly and carefully slip my clothes back on. I call out to my dad, letting him know that I'm awake again and that Jere might be coming over. I sit comfortably in my wheelchair and get warmed up with Jere's next text.

My Melissa,
They told me that to make her fall in love I had to make her laugh. But every time she laughs I'm the one who falls in love. Why do I have to pick you up, darling?

Jere

I grin and my heart jumps with joy. My dad comes upstairs and he pushed me downstairs into the living room. After settling down on the couch, I replied.

My Jere,
Forever is a long time. But, I wouldn't mind spending it by your side. You have to pick me up because Rosemary destroyed me on my first day back at school and now I'm in a wheelchair with a broken leg.

Melissa

I drop my phone on the couch and lay down. After about 10 minutes, I heard a light knock on the door. Before I could even lift my head in glee, my dad tells me to stay put as he answers the door. I laughed quietly once I heard what my dad had said. "Jeremiah Baldwin! So good to see you! How's your family? How was Georgia?" my dad booms once he opens the door. I hear Jere's laugh and my dad and laughs as well. Once I started dating him my dad loved him, and they've always been friends. Even before we were dating they were friends, all the way back since we entered 6th grade last year. At the time, so did Teresa.

"It's good seeing you too Mr. Logan. Umm, where's my Melissa?" He inquired sweetly. My dad chuckled and then whispered something to Jere that I couldn't quite make out before leading him over to me. We beamed once we saw each other and he gave me an enormous hug. My dad smiled as he set down Jere's makeup for math on the coffee table and ambled back to his office. Jere sat next to me and went right in for a kiss. I slowly leaned back as I moved my one hand through his soft, dirty blond hair and pushed my other hand across his cheek as he dragged me closer to him. Little by little we let go of each other, laughing as our foreheads bumped against each other. It felt really, really good to be with my boyfriend again.

I "jumped" in my wheelchair and Jere pushed me towards the door as my dad said to be back by 7:00. We giggled and talked all the way up to the park. He set up a picnic blanket on the meadow and we sat down in each other's arms. Jere suddenly sat up and looked down at me. Due to the fact that we've been dating for two years,

I could automatically tell that he wanted to talk about something concerning him.

"Your dad told me that you've had a hard time since I left. Is everything ok, Melissa?" Jere calmly asked. I roughly exhaled as I lay against his shoulder and I told him all about Teresa, the additions to the "Death Call", and what Rosemary did to me at school. He held me close as I shed both bitter and heartbroken tears into his arms. I dug inside my jean pocket and pulled out the piece of pottery that I kept. I put it in his open hand and he sat up to look at it.

"Melissa, isn't this is from you and Teresa's pot? You broke it?" Jere quietly exclaimed in disbelief. I nodded and told him about how I smashed it and threw the pot away but spared this piece's life. He looked at me in confusion and I sat up as well.

"I know it sounds weird that out of all of the pieces that I could've kept it was the one that said "I will always love you and be there for you.", but it helps remind me that we used to have something together." I admitted softly. Jere nodded and we settled back down on the blanket, holding each other once again. We talked, laughed and talked as the lovely time passed. After hysterically laughing for like 5 minutes, he turned around and softly touched his lips to mine. I lightly kissed him back while I wrapped my arms around him, bringing him in closer to me. Jere told me a joke and I held my head back laughing, as he dove in for another kiss and I returned the favor by lightly rubbing his back. After a few calm minutes, I suddenly gripped my leg in pain, wanting to sit in my wheelchair again. Jere lifted me onto my wheelchair and then all of a sudden, he got down on one knee. I covered my mouth with my hands in shock, starting to get emotional at what was probably about to happen, even though it was absolutely crazy. *I always knew Jere was crazy, but not this crazy.* I thought. By this point, Jere had taken out a small red velvet box and gestured for me to open it. I casually flipped open the box and I gasped as my flow of tears began to roll down my cheeks. Inside the box was a small sliver ring with an engraving of "My Melissa" on the outside, an engraving of "Endless Love" on the inside, and finally a diamond infinity symbol on the top. Jere took it out and held it out to me.

"Melissa, I love you, and I think I always will. I know this sounds crazy coming from a 7th grader, but I think I want to marry you, someday. This is a promise ring. I know that only high schoolers and adults do this kind of stuff, but if you wear it, I promise to love you, support you, and care for you in every situation possible. I promise to always be there for you and to cherish you. If at anytime that I don't do that, you can take it off. Maybe when we're a lot older and you're still wearing it, we can be together. Will you take this promise ring, Melissa?" Jere asked. I was now in total sob mode. I sat up and looked at his beautiful, charming, blue eyes.

"Yes, Jere. I will take your promise ring." I whispered. He smiled and slipped the beautiful promise ring on my left hand, ring finger. I fit me perfectly. Once the ring was on, I jumped into his arms and hugged him tightly. He hugged me tightly back while kissing the back of my neck. After a few moments of blurry eyes from crying, I saw someone slowly walking towards us. I froze and all of my muscles tensed up. **Rosemary**.

"Rosemary is walking right towards us. Go back to my house, I can hold her," I muttered, trying not to bring too much attention. Still hugging me, he grabbed my hand and squeezed it, and I knew that he wasn't going anywhere. I buried my head into his shoulder, my head aching from what might happen. Jere sighed back at me and slowly let go of me as he turned around to face Rosemary.

"Hello lovebirds. I'm pretty sure the couple night out was down the street at the Vesta dipping grill restaurant, not at the park. Get a room," Rosemary smirked as walked up to us. She looked down at me and tried to grab my wrist, but I quickly grabbed hers first and sharply twisted it backwards. She winced as her body started to bend backwards with her hand.

"What do you want, creep?" I snarled at her. I finally let go of her arm and she stumbled backwards. She chuckled and slowly raised her hands. A dim green glow started to form in Rosemary's hands and gather around Jere. Before anyone knew it, Jere was frozen and glowing green. I nudged him and tried to do something to shake him out of whatever Rosemary did, but it was no use. He didn't move one inch. Rosemary walked up to him and slapped him in the face. Hard. I was nearly about to punch her in the stomach, but hesitated, knowing what she could do to me with my very low use of defense.

"If you touch a hair on his head, I'll make sure your lovely body becomes a devil's omelet. Comprende?" I snapped. She sat down on the wet grass beside the blanket and shrugged. She then looked up at me and gave me a sad puppy face.

"Melissa! You're so mean. I don't have anyone to play with now," she mumbled, trying to sound as innocent as possible. I tugged my jean jacket over my mouth to muffle my laughter as I brought down my elbows so that they rested on my legs and gave her an innocent face as well.

"Well, I'm sorry Rosemary. You can play with me. Let's play patty cake and Monopoly! Gosh Rosemary, you're such a hypocrite," I sweetly explained which unintentionally turned into a snarl. She smiled and stood up again, sticking out one hand right at me. She started to close her head into a fist, while I started to slowly rise into the air.

"I love that idea! Let's play Monopoly, "Death Call" style! I'll go first. I buy Melissa Logan for her boo!" Rosemary sourly sang as I rose higher and higher. I screamed and told her not to touch him and to put me down, but she just ignored me. She quickly jutted her fist inwards towards her chest. I sped towards her and in one heartbeat, I was sitting next to her evil polka dot heels in chains. She sighed and looked down at me.

"Well, time for the banker, me, to get me my money," Rosemary laughed as she showed her green gleam and unfroze Jere. He stumbled forward and stood silent for a minute until he realized what was going on.

"Melissa! Rosemary, let her go." Jere said calmly, but you could tell from a far distance that he was red in the face with anger at Rosemary at the fact that his girlfriend was chained up. Rosemary giggled and took a breath to summarize the situation.

"Jeremiah! Nice to hear from you again! Well, here's what has happened. Melissa screamed at me, then I pouted at her, they I stood up and decided we should play Monopoly "Death Call" style, and then I bought Melissa in exchange for you!" Rosemary explained calmly, as if nothing was wrong. I struggled against the chains until Rosemary grabbed my usable foot and glared at me. With one look, I stopped moving and stayed still. Jere breathed in slowly and sat down in my wheelchair while Rosemary slowly walked around him, dragging me easily with her end of the chain.

"So, since I bought your darling with you as cash, I'm going to ask you to make a choice," Rosemary requested, "you can either try to save your truelove and risk extreme danger from me, or you can leave your honey here and go back home," Rosemary ended, proudly ending her 360 tour right in front of Jere. *Jere needs to leave. I'm not going to watch him get hurt. I'll be fine, right? Jere said he'll support me if I wore his ring, so...* I thought. Before either of them could say anything, I talked to Jere.

"Jere, go home, or go to my house. I don't want you to get hurt. I can handle her," I said, trying to confront him but only to fail when Rosemary yanked me back to her. Tears appeared in Jere's eyes and I knew he wouldn't do it. He rose from the wheelchair and with caution, started to walk towards me.

"I'll be fine, Melissa. I'm not leaving this park without you," Jere answered unsteadily. He took another step towards me and Rosemary immediately acted. She crossed her fingers and pointed towards Jere. An invisible force rammed into Jere and shoved him to the ground. Without thinking, I looked at my watch. 6:50. Jere had to get back to the house and tell my dad I'm ok. I pressed my fingers against and around my promise ring and stared at Jere.

"Jeremiah Edward Baldwin! I want you to go home to my father right now. If you don't," I whispered, "I will take off my promise ring. You said you would always support me, and you'll do that if you leave," I cried as I gripped my ring with all my might. Jere continued to cry but smiled at me. He gave a evil glare at Rosemary for a moment, and then started walking back to my house. I started crying and almost wanted to scream at him to come back, because I knew he will. But I didn't. I wiped my eyes and stared at the ground, ready to make Rosemary pay yet again.

"Well, that was ridiculous. It's your turn in Monopoly. What does little wannabe here want?" Rosemary sighed as she stared me down. I stared right back at her and suddenly saw something move. I locked my eyes on it and saw that Jere didn't fully leave. He was hiding behind a bush right near the downhill path to my house. He was doing hand and feet motions, like he was playing charades. If we were playing charades, he was telling me to somehow kick or punch Rosemary hard enough to get on my wheelchair and roll down to him. I rubbed my forehead in concern, realizing how dangerous and insane that was. But before I did anything, Rosemary released me from my chains and bent down to face me.

"I know I've been a **real** pain in the butt lately, and I'm sorry. If I had a choice, I would want to be friends with you and your crew, play on the basketball team, and have nothing to do with the Death Call," Rosemary admitted under her breath. I stared at her in disbelief. I'm guessing she saw my expression as she continued to explain her confession.

"I was someone who made up the same game at my old school, like you and Amber. My friend and I were so close to breaking the curse and the "Death Call" got furious. It increased the curse on my school and hypnotized me into being on the game's side to stop other people from breaking the curse," she whispered. I really wanted to think that she was lying, but somehow I believed her. I could see in her eyes all the times I've been against her a slight sign of guilt, fear, and maybe kindness. I had to suddenly make a split second decision. Either don't believe her, hit her and roll to Jere, or believe her and help her. I decided to do both.

"I believe you, Rosemary. But Jeremiah won't, yet. If you trust me, meet me after basketball practice on Monday. If you are truly for defeating the "Death Call", my crew will understand. Now, pretend that I punched you in the stomach," I murmured urgently. After a moment of consideration, she nodded. I nodded back, and she suddenly threw herself unto the ground while holding her stomach in "agony". I quickly hobbled over to my wheelchair and rolled as fast as I could over to Jere. He quickly grabbed the handlebars and raced me down to my house just after 7. We rushed into my room and collapsed unto my half circle love couch. We finally decided that we could breath and giggled as we relaxed into each other's arms. After watching a episode of F.R.I.E.N.D.S while eating chocolate and popcorn, it was time for Jere to head out.

"Sorry I threatened to take off my promise ring if you didn't leave. I know you were trying to just protect me," I whispered in his ear while I hugged him. All he did was hold me closely and leaned in closer to my ear.

"I'm so glad threatened to take it off. You were trying to protect me. I'm glad the ring is still on though," Jere whispered back. He turned towards me and lightly kissed me. I smiled as I accepted and wrapped my arms around him.

A few minutes later, Jere was gone and I was laying on my bed, drifting into my sleep. Right before I closed my eyes, I heard a ding on my computer. I ambled out of bed and saw a new email in my inbox. I would think it was one of my friends, or Mrs.Genie, or even Rosemary, but it was none other than Teresa.

Melissa,
Hey. I just want you to hear me out, ok? I would **never** kidnap your brothers and use you and your father. I want to be with you guys. Do you trust me? Please email me back, whether you trust me or not. Good night sweetheart.

Teresa

       I have no idea what to say, but I know that I have a lot to think about. Even though there are plenty of things that suspect that she's totally lying, Teresa has never lied to me, to us before.

Teresa,
I don't know, yet.

Melissa

Monday, April 9, 2018.
6:07 in the morning.

       I gradually wake up after a lousy Sunday and feel super relieved for some reason. I'm about to call my dad to help me get up when I sit up and look at my legs. My broken leg has no cast on it, and when I move it I feel fine. *I'm not supposed to get my cast off for another 5 weeks! Where is it?*

I thought. Another thing, my wheelchair and crutches are gone. I pick up my phone and find a text from the one and only Rosemary, who happened to have my number.

Melissa,
I forgot to tell you. "The Death Call" gave me a one time wish for helping him, or it. I made it a two in one. Like your restored leg? I bet Amber likes her arm back too. See you at school…

Rosemary

I looked at the text in disbelief but I quickly jump up in joy, feeling both of my legs fill up with adrenaline. I got dressed, packed up my clothes for basketball, and ran downstairs. My dad jumped with fright when he saw me walking with no sign of pain from my face as I grabbed some waffles. I ignored his confused face and kissed him goodbye, yelling to him that I'm walking to school as I closed the door and started my morning walk. I met up with Amber and saw with no surprise that her broken arm was healed, just like Rosemary said.

"Melissa? Amber?!" I heard multiple people yell as Amber and I got to a stop sign. We turned around to see all of our friends looking at us in shock and awe at the obvious notice of our healed limbs. After we confirmed that we were not playing with them, they screamed with glee and ran towards us in a big group hug. We all walked to school hand and hand as we talked about our weekends, including Jere's return, our Rosemary encounter and how she healed Amber and I. We laughed with so much intensity that we all bumped into Mrs. Genie, who was a huge barrier in the hallway, staring down at us with the most evil glares that I have ever seen.

"Melissa! Amber! Girls!" Mrs. Genie said with a happy _and_ disappointed tone, as if she was delighted yet horrified that we came to school.

"I see that you girls are already fully healed from last Friday's accident. Lucky, lucky," she murmured as she leaned towards us. All of a sudden, Mrs. Eagle called Mrs. Genie over to the front office computer and while she turned her head, we sped down the hall and straight to our lockers. I don't know what happened, but everyone moved over to the walls once we got to the middle school hallway, giving me and my girls the walk-a-way to our lockers. Jere was at the end of the hall, and I giggled at the sight of him gawking at the fact that I was walking. I ran towards him and hugged him as tight as I could. After he realized that he could embrace me, he hugged me back and rocked me slowly back and forth. Suddenly, Jere stopped hugging me and snapped his fingers. Trent and Gavin grabbed me by my arms and roughly dragged me behind Jere. Once I finally got them off of me, I looked above Jere's shoulder and immediately realized why I'm behind him. At the end of the hall stood the lovely Rosemary Raven. She cracked a smile and waved at me. I slightly smiled back at her, knowing I needed to break the tension between everyone and her. I used all my might to push through Jere and before he could stop me, I jogged over to Rosemary with all the shocked eyes following me.

"Hey," I said. She smiled and reached out for a hug. I accepted, and it felt good. Everyone probably thought I was crazy, but in this moment, I didn't care.

"Hey. I'm sorry about the whole breaking bones thing last week. Hope you forgive me. You too Amber," Rosemary announced and pointed to Amber. Amber smiled and ran out to us and gave us a bear hug. We giggled and everyone lost interest, starting to open their lockers and get to class. Once I sat down in Spanish and showed Rosemary what to do for the do now and where to sit, I felt a light touch on the shoulder. I turned around and saw Jere staring down at me. I thought he was going to scream or yell at me or maybe even take off his promise ring, but he just smiled. I smiled back. He left to go back to his table with Rosemary when a sticky note fell out of his back pocket. I was about to call him back when I saw my name on it. I picked it up and was grinning with happiness when I finished reading it.

Melissa,
You were so brave this morning. At first, I was really confused, but then I found out about your talk with Rosemary last night. You are being so kind to her by giving her a

second chance, and that is the one of the exact reasons why I asked you out in the first place.

Love ya,
Jere

      I put the note away and started working on my project. I thought that for now, everything is fine and pure. Rosemary and Jere were already friends, and the whole crew (now including Rosemary) is now whole and happy. For some nasty reason, however, those exact moments are when everything comes crashing down. I hear the door open to the classroom and everyone's head turn. I hear the front office woman call for Rosemary, Jere, and I. I see the three of us being stared at as we walk towards the door. I feel pain and loads of concern when I hear that Teresa wants to see all of us at her house after school, no exceptions. I hear the bell announce the end of class, and see my classmates rush for the door.

      For the rest of the day, everything was just a blur for me, my whole life kinda exploding like TNT around me. Right after I get something good, three really bad things follow. I had no idea what this meant, what was going to happen, and if things will change between the three of us or any of us. At the end of the day, I confirmed that basketball practice was cancelled due to Ms.Eagle's sickness and that practice was tomorrow. What a coincidence! I walked towards Rosemary and Jere at the front of the school and grabbed their hands, holding them close.

"So, where is this Teresa's house, Melissa?" Rosemary smirked. Jere and I smirked back as we looked at each other. After one smile between the three of us, I squeezed their hands and I lead them out on the sidewalk and onto Teresa's house.

Once we got there, I already wanted to turn around and run. Even though I have lived with this woman for most of my life, there is still the huge fact that she decided to pack her stuff and peace out. Let's also not forget the not so good and scary threats she made in my house just a few days ago. Besides that, we slowly walked towards the door and with all my fright, I banged on the door. The door opened a moment later and Teresa's grin got wider and wider as she saw us.

"Melissa, Jeremiah, and Rosemary. Thank you for coming! Come inside," Teresa acknowledged as she stepped back to let us all in. We walked in and stared intensely at her walls as Jere took our jackets and hung them up. Teresa giggled anxiously as she lead us into her basement with her first, then Jere, then me and finally Rosemary trailing behind.

Once we were all down the steep stairs, Teresa grinned and turned on the lights. I was shocked to see that there were only three pieces of furniture in the large basement. Standing in a triangle formation were three big black chairs that were all facing the front of the room and had some holding things on the arms. After a few moments of staring at how weird this was, we totally forgot about Teresa and spun around only to be attacked by... washcloths.

A FEW MINUTES LATER...

I wake up by the sound of loud moaning and groaning. Painful moaning and groaning. I open one eye and see that my hand is enclosed by chains, (which are attached to the black chair I saw earlier), and saw Jere locked up in another chair. While opening my other eye, I saw my other hand, Rosemary locked in one chair, and Teresa sitting in a normal chair at the front. I wanted to scream at her but no words came out. I felt around in my mouth and got more mad when realizing that there was a thick washcloth stuck in my mouth. I watched with anger as Jere and Rosemary started to wake up and go through the same realizations that I did. After Teresa saw that we were all caught up, she stood up and started to walk around us.

"Well then, let me just take these washcloths out of your mouths and then we can have a little chat," Teresa sighed as she one by one plucked them out of our mouths. After throwing them in the trash and sitting back in her seat, she leaned in and plastered on her serious face.

"Look, here's the deal. I'm sick of the three of you being friends and working together to stop all of this," Teresa said quickly but stopped abruptly when I lifted my finger.

"Before you continue your very scary speech Teresa, let me remind you that the three of us have been friends for less than a whole day. Second of all, we haven't been able to defeat the

"Death Call" because we've been busying figuring Rosemary out and dealing with our own lives," I argued.

"Great job, Melissa! I always knew you had a least a segment of a brain. I already knew all of that. After our interesting conversation that involved the police, I realized that I don't need you, and I never will. I have joined the "Death Call". So I'm not under force like Rosemary was. The "Death Call" has asked me to do him a favor," Teresa hinted.

"He saw that Melissa here has always found a way to get through the barriers. She got through Rosemary, me, and lots of others. He noticed that all of this happened partly, because she was supported. He wants to take that away from you," Teresa giggled as I stiffened in my chair. I knew that she wanted to separate me from the people I love. But what I couldn't understand is why Rosemary and Jere are with me when it's my fate.

"Will you just get on with it?" Jere groaned after a long not needed moment of silence. Teresa pointed her finger at him she started to babble all over again.

"Once I was given this task, I had to find the perfect person to separate her from. I was driving past the park right near here last week and saw Melissa and Jeremiah. I was just going to ignore you two and continue my way when I saw Jeremiah putting a ring on Melissa's finger. I immediately knew that it was a promise ring. I thought that was just so sweet because things like that are sweet and I had found the perfect way to destroy

Melissa," Teresa sighed with a grin. I felt a tear appearing on my cheek but I couldn't wipe it off. Teresa walked over to a panel and firmly pressed a button. Jere and Rosemary's chairs started to rotate and move closer to each other until they were facing each other and were inches apart.

"So what are you going to do? Find some crazy way to break Jeremiah and Melissa up? You're insane to think that's even possible. I've seen them together. Nothing could ever break them apart," Rosemary complained. Teresa just shook her head and walked towards us. After considering whatever she wanted to say, she cleared her throat to say the most horrifying thing I have ever heard her say.

"Melissa, remember a few nights ago when you had all of your nightmares except your worst nightmare?" Teresa suddenly asked. I looked at her in total confusion of why and how she knew that, but nodded.

"Well, that was the "Death Call" looking into your mind to find your worst nightmare. That's why you saw all of your nightmares except your worst one. The "Death Call" showed this worst nightmare to me and that's exactly what I'm going to do to you. To all of you. Now Melissa, tell your friends what that nightmare is so that they're prepared," Teresa chuckled, poking me on the arms as she stood behind me. I just sat there, shocked at what she was going to do to me, to us. Jere and Rosemary leaned in towards me, urging me to say something.

"The day I first met Rosemary, I had my worst nightmare. I dreamt that since Rosemary was so beautiful and she had very strong powers, I had a nightmare that Rosemary will get Jere's attention and that Jere will leave me for her. This nightmare faded away when Jere gave me my promise ring, but it's still there," I breathed, tears streaking my face. Jere was tearing up as well, and Rosemary was struggling to breath as she realized what was going to happen. Teresa was still behind me and I could tell that she was holding in laughter. She walked back around and stood at the front of the room.

"Great summary Melissa! So here's what's going to go down. I'm going to take Melissa's promise ring. Then Jeremiah is going to give Rosemary Melissa's promise ring just like Jere did with Melissa, and Melissa is going to watch," Teresa snarled. Jere immediately went into his shell, holding his body close. Rosemary exploded with anger and tried her hardest to get out of the chair, tears streaming down her face as she watched the two of us crumble. I just went straight into tears, so scared of what was about to happen. The worst part of the nightmare wasn't the fact that Jere was taken from me, but that I had to watch it happen. I wiped my tears and tried shoving down the rest.

"Mom, please. Please don't do it," I cried and screamed, "please don't take him away from me, mom." Teresa looked at me and I suddenly saw that she was crying too. She's being controlled, like Rosemary was. She didn't want to do it. She quickly wiped her tear and with the swish of her finger, my ring was ripped off of my finger and into her hands. I dropped my head into my lap but my head was soon picked up by a machine and was held there as Jere gave Rosemary her ring and they both said what was needed to be said. With one more grief smile, Teresa pressed one more button and left the room. The chains were released and I fell straight to the ground in tears. Jere was there just in time to catch me and I sobbed in his arms. Rosemary ran over to us and all of us just cried in each other's arms. After a while, we left and walked by ourselves home. Once I opened the door to the house and my dad saw me, he knew something was wrong.

I just held my hand that had the ring up and whispered Teresa. My dad got the memo and I cried in his arms all over again. We ate some ice cream and pizza and I cried myself to sleep.

Tuesday, April 10, 2018.
7:55 in the morning.

The next morning, I decided to focus on other things. All of me and Rosemary's friends and Jere's friends knew about what happened. They also knew that the three of us didn't want to talk about it. So when Jere, Rosemary, and I walked to school, everyone just thought happy thoughts and talked about happy things. But all of us got right back to that depressing stage when we all read Teresa's email on my laptop in homeroom.

Melissa,
Before you read the rest, I want you to know that I would never do that to you and Jeremiah. I am being controlled. This is a message from the Death Call:

I'm warning you Melissa. If you or any of your friends try to end Jeremiah and Rosemary's relationship, real pain will head your way.

Teresa

My head filled with rage as it sunk in what the deal was. *There is a threat to the three of us now? Does Jere and Rosemary have to go on dates now? What does that mean for me?* I thought. All I knew right now is that if I stayed away from Rosemary and Jere, I won't have as much water as the ocean. If I stay away from Teresa, I won't hear the voice, (which has disappeared for like a couple of days now.)

I slammed my laptop closed with fury and rushed to Spanish class as the bell rang. I spent the rest of Spanish, Language Arts and Elective class so outraged and heartbroken, ignoring everyone I wanted to be with. But Jere isn't used to this; I usually come to him or my friends when I'm upset. So during recess, he finally decided to confront me.

"Melissa! What is up with you today? I know things are hard right now, but I want to hang out with you," Jere admitted. I sighed, turned around, and kept on walking.

"Where are you going after school, Jeremiah?" I asked as my footsteps slowed down to a stop, my voice hoarse after calling Jere **Jeremiah**.

"I'm going on a date with Rosemary," Jere whispered.

"Yeah, that's what I thought. Have fun," I mutter as I continue walking.

"Wait, Melissa! Please, just hang out with me. I'm only going on a date with Rosemary so the "Death Call" doesn't hurt any of us," Jere pleaded. He ran towards me and once he touched my arm, all of my feelings exploded inside of me like the finale of fireworks on July 4th as I whipped around to face him.

"Don't you get it Jere! I want hang out with you so bad, run into your arms and hold you close but I can't," I cried, wiping tears from my eyes.

"Every time I look at you, or talk to you, all I think is that I can't be with you. It kills me, kills me! I will always be with you and only you. But until we figure this out, just stay away, ok?" I pleaded as I ran away. Once I got to the playground, I turned around to look at him, and he was watching me. I wanted to reach out to him and tell him everything was going to be alright, but I couldn't.

The rest of the day was a haze of sadness and disappointment. I was purposely isolated and it made me feel horrible. I told Ms. Eagle that I won't be attending practice and Rosemary probably won't go either, even though I really wanted to play. It's not like it mattered anyway, Ms. Eagle responded by kicking Rosemary and I off the team since we have never been to practice and apparently missed two games. Not to mention the Voice's return as well! I got to hear this all day and it was not good.

After school today, you will live in darkness, total darkness. After school today, you will live in darkness, total darkness. After school today, you will live in darkness, total darkness…

I later told my dad I needed fresh air and I decided to walk home. Almost at my house and aching to just rest, I see Teresa's house in the distance. I don't have any homework, so I walked a little longer and firmly knocked on the door. Teresa opened the door and her face immediately when into shock and panic mode. I didn't know what to say, so I just started out casual.

"Hey, Teresa. How are you? Can we talk?" I sighed, trying to sound as calm as possible since I'm shaking inside out. I don't know why I was here, she just broke my heart yesterday. But here I was. She scanned my eyes for a while until she finally nodded.

"Sure. But come in quickly. The "Death Call" can't see us together," Teresa answered quickly, pulling me in and locking the door behind her. I had no idea what I was doing, but I assumed that her basement was the safest place. I quickened to drop my jacket and backpack and race downstairs. As soon as we got down there and we were safely inside, I wanted to get right back out. It's horrible to spend the whole day not seeing your boyfriend/ex boyfriend, but it's even worse when you're where it all started.

This time, the basement was set up like a normal basement. It had two couches, a TV, a bathroom, and a mini kitchen area. I sat down on the couch and before I could even think, immediately confronted Teresa.

"Teresa, I want you to come back. I know you haven't meant anything you've said or done the past few weeks. I just can't let you in when you're being controlled. Can I help you with that?" I confessed, talking really fast and tightly holding onto my fingers. Teresa definitely seemed shocked by this, but seemed very happy as well.

"I would love that Melissa. Is your dad ok with that? Like, does he know about all of this?" Teresa questioned, almost as if she didn't believe me. I slightly nodded as my heartbeat started to finally slow. After a minute of thought, she nodded as well.

"Ok then. I saw Rosemary when she was released from the "Death Call", and I believe that you have to say the situation you regret the most and what you would've done differently," I mumbled, hoping that she wouldn't get mad. It has always been hard for us to share what we regretted. Now, it's especially when it's about each other. She shifted in her seat at the awkward silence, but I saw in her eyes that she wanted this so much.

"What I regret the most is leaving you," Teresa sighed. I sat stone still in my seat, not knowing what to say. I just, didn't understand why this is her most regretted moment. She has already told me all of this. She said this when she first visited me, but she wasn't released.

"Before I continue, I have to tell something. Your dad and I wanted to wait until you were 16, but you need to know now. I'm... I'm not your real mother," Teresa admitted, holding her hands so tight that they were quickly turned to ghost white. In that moment, I wanted to be so angry at her and everything, but instead I felt really miserable. Tears immediately left my eyes, my arms wrapped around my suddenly aching and rocking body. Teresa sighed deeply and wrapped her present in her wrapping paper as we sat there It took a moment before I was calm and Teresa could continue.

"A week after you were born, your mother and your father were at the subway. I was there too, heading downtown for a meeting. They were in each other's arms, fully in love with you and only you. A few minutes before the train got to the station, a group of people came down and all the lights went off. There was screaming and yelling everywhere, all around me. When all the lights went back on, half of the people were kidnapped by the group, including your mother," Teresa confessed, choking at almost every word. I had know idea why I was crying, but I was creating a lake onto Teresa's shoulders and I couldn't stop it.

"Everyone left or called 911 immediately. I was about to leave in horror, when I saw your dad. He was crying and holding you close in his arms, your mother's purse beside him. I wanted to be nice, so I helped him up and I stayed at his place for a while. I took care of you and him until he was ready to hold down the fort himself. We didn't see each other for a few months after that, but once your dad put what happened beside, he and I had a spark. We got married when you were 10 months old," Teresa said, slightly smiling at the thought. As Teresa told this story, I suddenly realized that I missed her so much. I let her continue to hold me and for once, I didn't feel alone.

"I regret leaving you because you didn't have a mother. I was there for you only a week after you were born, caring for you and falling in love with you and your father. You were my family and I left all of that because I thought that was not enough. But you, your dad, Marvin and Gale are all I could ever want," Teresa slowly continued, "you should go home now." I wiped the last of the tears from my eyes and grabbed her hand.

"Let's go home. Together," I smiled. She grinned and we dashed upstairs, down the street and up to my house. We ran up to the door and my dad answered on the first knock, suddenly looking shocked and concerned. But in that moment, we all understood each other. He started crying and gently grabbed Teresa into a tight hug. She started crying as well and held him and I close. We slowly went inside the house and Teresa and I told him that I learned about my real mother and the subway story. Instead of being upset that I was told early, he grinned and embraced both of us. As we finally started to breathe and settle in our seats, he took my hands in his.

"Melissa, there's one more thing I, we have to tell you," my dad admitted, "your mom escaped from that group and is now ok, and you know your mom. You've met her already, you just haven't known," my dad finished, apparently trying to go slow so I can hear it all clearly. For some reason, I got really excited that my mom was still alive and in my life, but I just didn't know until now.

"Really? Who is she? I've met her before? Who is my mother?" I asked quickly, fidgeting in my seat. My dad slightly smiled and I realized that my mother might be someone I don't like in my life.

"Your mother is Ms.Genie," my dad mumbled. I stared back at him in pure shock, all of my hope crashing down into a deep dark gap that never seemed to stop. I yanked my hand away from dad, grabbing my bag and running out of the door. I ran straight to Jere's house, even though he is basically one of the last people I wanted to see. Jere was sitting on the porch when I got there; his date with Rosemary was probably short. When he saw me crying, he ran towards me to hold me close. It felt so good, and I cried even harder because I missed this. Missed us. We sat on the porch and after a while, I told him that Teresa is not my mom, but Ms. Genie is. There was no conversation other than that. We just held each other, not letting each other go.

After a while, I told him that I had to go back home, and we just said a simple goodbye. It was difficult to go home, but quickly I got my dinner and went straight to my room. I felt like I was living in so much darkness, total darkness. The Voice was right. Right now, I'm just surrounded in so much hurt, so much pain. I haven't have had time to worry about the "Death Call", since I've had to deal with my mess of a life, which was crumbling apart. Now almost a whole grade is gone, and we need to do something right away.

Wednesday, April 11, 2018.
7:34 in the morning.

The next morning, I went straight to school with my breakfast and without any knowledge of my dad or Teresa, who apparently spent the night. I walked into the building with Abree but left her as I walked straight into Ms. Genie's office. I threw my backpack on the carpet and slammed her office door behind me, my eyes deepened with anger and my mind set on only this. Only her.

"You knew that I was your daughter?! All this time?" I screamed at her. I was already so angry that she was even my mom in the first place. Even more that she was never there for me and that she hasn't said anything after 7 years of me being a student here. Point obvious also, why didn't my dad get back with her when he found out she was alive and ok?

"Hey sweetheart. I-" Ms. Genie started, trying earnestly to calm me down. But I was only taken aback when she said "sweetheart". *She was only in my life for a week and she thinks she has a right to call me that.* I thought.

"Don't you dare call me sweetheart, you were only with me for a week! What happened?" I retorted, sitting in the chair before I fully turned into a exploding nuke. She grimaced but slowly told me what happened. Soon after, I left the room leaving no regards for her time. Jere obviously told everyone close to me (including Rosemary) about what happened and when they heard that I talked to Ms. Genie, they were dying to know what she said.

"She told me that the story that my parents told me is true. Said that when she was kidnapped, she had the option to go back to her family for some reason or leave her family. She decided to a start a new life. She got the principal job here and when she held interviews, my dad was there," I muttered, trying my hardest to keep my cool.

"They talked and he told her about Teresa and they decided that it would be best to stay separate and give full custody of me to my dad. Teresa and my dad got married two months after that," I hissed, still very enraged with everyone in my family. Everyone reminded me to keep my anger on the low side, but the rest of the day was still very hard. Lucky, nobody mentioned the situation, but over half of the middle school now knew that I was Ms. Genie's daughter. Everyone knows that I'm not a cruel and scary person, but knowing there are basically "two Ms. Genies" roaming the school is pretty creepy.

Today was so messed up, all I could do during pick up is sigh. Just like everyday, someone was taken. It was Abree today. I cried and since I was vowed on independence, all I could do was cry and hold myself. To add on to all the frustration, Ms. Genie emailed me right when I got back home, right when I thought I was safe from everything, anything.

Melissa,
I'm so sorry that all of this happened. I want to talk this out with you and really meet you so that we don't live our lives "not knowing each other". Please email me back.

Your mom/principal,
Ms. Genie (Amy)

I was so confused by this email. I really was not in the mood to meet the **second** mom that abandoned me. So after pulling on my pjs and strength, I emailed her back.

Ms. Genie/ "mom",

I'm sorry too. I just don't understand how you get kidnapped, get the chance to go back to your family and decide to leave them. You ditched us for a "fresh start". I was a week old, I was your fresh start; your new phase in your life! Then you see that I'm a student here and you don't say anything until I'm in 7th grade. I've been here for 7 years! I understand that you're my birth mom, but you are definitely not in the mom category for me. "Mother, one who loves and cares for her children; to watch over, nourish, and protect." That is **_not_** you, and as far as I'm convinced, you will never be. Have a great night Ms. Genie/ "mom".

Melissa

        I finally relaxed and I went downstairs to get a snack and check on dad. He asked me if I would be ok letting Teresa move back in, and I said of course. I explained that I was just upset about Ms. Genie, but I was ecstatic about Teresa finally coming back. As I watched tv with dad, I felt as if I'm finally in my calm place, for now. After dinner, I went back to my room to notice an envelope on my bed.

My Melissa,
I want to see you again. Meet me at the park and make sure no one comes with you.

Jere

It was only 6:30, so I let my dad know and I was headed to the park. I was surprised that he wanted to see me after I yelled and cried at him, but was still happy as I ran to the park.

When I got there, Jere was waiting for me with a bouquet of my favorite flowers, purple and white tulips. I ran towards him and he bowed as he gave me the flowers.

"What's this? I thought we weren't supposed to be together and you're supposed to be with Rosemary," I smiled yet sighed. Jere nodded, stood up and looked into my eyes longingly.

"I really wanted to see you anyway, but I got a note that you wanted to see me at the park so I decided to buy you your favorite flowers," Jere answered. I looked at him like he was joking, but noticed that he was telling the truth. I shook my head and took his hand in mine.

"I wanted to see you too, but I got a note saying that you wanted to see me and meet you at the park." I replied. Someone was playing us, but I honestly didn't care. I gently put the flowers down and took both of his hands, grinning. We were together, and that's all that mattered to me. I leaned in and in one second we were kissing like we were together, like everything was normal. We slowly let go and watched the sunset until someone started to approach us. I let go of Jere and went up to this tall suspicious boy, probably around our age.

"Were you the one who played us? Not like we're mad, but still," I inquired, since he did walk up to us. He smirked and started to slowly walk around us. I instantly went beside Jere, still staring intensely at this boy.

"Oh, I didn't do it," he admitted with innocent hands, "It's your mom that did it, Melissa." I was in stock, but only for a couple of moments.

"Ok, slow down. Three things. One, how do you know me, my name? Two, who the heck are you? Three, why did my mother do this, even though she is acting like a jerk at the moment?" I questioned, studying his movements and his face to see if I knew him. He stopped in front of us and before I knew it, he pushed Jere really hard against a rock filled with ivy and the ivy started to wrap itself around him, quickly.

"My name is Shane Genie, your brother. Obviously I know you because you're my sister, mom talks about you all the time. She did this so that you and Jeremiah would be caught breaking the "getting back together" rule. So now, you deal with the "Death Call" punishment," he answered as he walked even closer to me.

Inside I was overwhelmed with all of these questions and some shocking concerns, so I was only able to mutter, "What punishments?" He laughed and snatched my flowers away from me.

"You're going to visit the "Death Call"," Shane hissed into my ear. As if on cue, the wind started blowing really hard and it "wrapped" around me, attaching to parts of my body. I was lifted into the air as Shane waved a happy wave towards me. I screamed for Jere but got pulled out of the park too quickly.

I was "flying", and as I went, I was getting faster and faster. I had to close my eyes at the intense wind around me, and when I opened my eyes every so often, it was pitch black. Moments later, my body felt ground and some source of light hit my face. I groaned and blocked the light with my hand, long enough to see where I am. Looking around, it was a big large room, with multiple scared little kids glancing at me and hallways stretching in all directions. I immediately assumed that this was the "Death Call" liar or something.

"Melissa?!" A gasp rose in my throat and I turned around from where I was sitting. Huddled together in a corner, Marvin and Gale sat there, staring at me intently with hope.

"Marvin! Gale!" I exclaimed, standing up and running towards them. I barricaded into them and we surrounded each other with hugs and kisses. I started crying and once I got a hold of them, I didn't let go.

"I missed you guys so much. You have no idea," I cried, smiling at them and holding them even tighter. If this were any other day, we would be trying so hard to get away from each other. But today, all we wanted is to be together and in each other's arms. After a few seconds, Marvin slowly sat back up.

"How's you and dad? I know this sounds weird, but have you've seen Teresa lately?" Marvin quietly asked, hoping that I wouldn't kill him for even mentioning her. I nodded and told them about her, about how Ms. Genie is my mom and that Teresa just moved back in. Just the thought of all of it was so warming to all three of us. But I didn't tell them about Shane. I just didn't know what to think of him, yet.

"Hey, do you guys know where Faye or Abree is?" I asked, hoping that I could talk to her about kinda everything. Gale pointed off to a darkened corner, deserted.

"Faye talked to us a little when she got here and is in the "in" crowd around here, but the rest of the time she has just sat there or in her room during our free time, alone," Gale explained softly. I thanked him and slowly walked towards Faye. I kneeled closely behind her reached to hug her from behind. Faye shuddered sharply, turned around and was about to shrug me off when she saw my face.

"Hey Faye. It's me," I cried. Faye immediately started to cry as she wrapped her arms around me. I pulled her close and held her as we rocked back in forth in her corner of tears. After she calmed down, I couldn't help but ask what it's like here.

"Well, it's like a boarding school. You share a room with three other people. You wake up and school is at 7:00. I suggest you wake up at 6:00, so you have time to get ready and walk to the building. School ends at 4. Then you have homework and free time. There's breakfast, lunch, and dinner in the cafeteria and curfew is at 10:30," Faye shrugs, acting like everything is fine. I smiled at the fact that everything was technically alright for her and the boys.

Just then, a keychain with keys dropped into my lap. Seconds later there was a schedule, a map, blankets & a pillow, bathroom things, and a backpack with all my school supplies next to me. One of the keys were written *Room: R25.* The other said *Locker 7*. I assumed that one was the key to my room and the other was the key to my locker.

Suddenly, kids started standing up around me and walking towards another hallway that must be the way to all the dorm rooms. Faye told me she'll see me tomorrow and quickly walked away to her room. I looked at my map and lead myself all the way at the end of the hall. I unlocked the door, walked in and saw two girls and a guy standing beside their beds. One girl immediately gave me sour eyes and pointed at the end of the room. There was a empty bed with a dresser and a small bookshelf. I slightly smiled and silently started to put the little that I had into places. After sitting down and giving my body a rest, the boy came over and sat on my chair near my bed. I studied him and pointed out in my mind his dirty blond hair, just like Jere's, that collided with his hazel eyes. If I wasn't distracted by where I am and the fact that I have a boyfriend, he's really cute.

"Hi, I'm Alexander. The girl in the yellow dress over there is Sabrine, and that girl that gave you sour eyes is Ember. What's your name?" Alexander wondered. I smiled, and although I honestly didn't trust any of these people, I had a good feeling about Alexander.

"My name is Melissa. Um, can someone please give me a little info on all of this? Everything?" I pleaded. Alexander smirked and looked as if he was about to answer, but Ember pushed him off the armless chair and sat herself down.

"Ok Melissa. You set up your clothes and all the stuff you need on that tablet next to your bed. There's a alarm that wakes us up and you'll be your own tour guide at school tomorrow. Will discuss everything else during lunch, got it?" Ember snapped. I was speechless and just nodded. She nodded and went back to her reading on her own chair. I didn't even bother to see what Alexander did next because I was busy looking at the tablet sitting in front of me.

This tablet was now my personal tablet here and it asked me all these questions to set up all my clothes and the things I liked to do. I pressed the finish button and suddenly a box with my name on it had all the clothes I ordered and the activities I liked to do on my bed. After a few minutes of playing *Subway Surfers*, a loud bell started ringing in all of the rooms. Before I could even ask, Ember said that the bell meant lights out. I snuggled into my pjs and without a single word, I brushed my teeth in our bathroom, turned off my lamp and got in bed. I started crying silently because I was so afraid of all of this and all I was thinking about was my family and how I would kill to be with all of them right now.

Thursday, April 12, 2018.
6:01 in the morning.

I woke up to the sounds of a very annoying alarm that I'm guessing is in the far corner of the room and Ember's croaking voice that Sabrine will look over my schedule with me and then I'm on my own for the day. I just nodded and slowly stumbled out of my bed. I decided to go with a silk white top, ripped light blue jeans, and my hair braided out for the day. After almost 10 minutes of staring at everyone else, they were all ready to go.

"Well, I'll go over your schedule with you and then I'll let you go, ok?" Sabrine requested as she grabbed her backpack. I nodded and as we all walked out of the dorm building, grabbed yogurts and granola bars for breakfast, and through the gloomy yet sunny day, she explained my schedule.

"Ok. You have Social Studies first in room 349, then you have Spanish in room 375, after that you have Math in room 320. Then you have recess and near the playground is the food court for lunch. Then you have your free period. After that you have Science in room 509. Last you have L.A which is in room 460. Any questions?" Sabrine explained. I felt like I shouldn't have any questions, but I asked them anyway.

"Two questions. Where do you go during free period and can we see anyone during our free period?" I asked. She smiled and lead me closer to the entrance.

"During free period, you can do what you want, as long as you stay in either in the school building or in the dormitories. Yes, you can hang with people that have free period with you," Sabrine said, "your brother Marvin has free period the same time you do. I can tell him you want to hang with him during free period?" Sabrine grinned, pointing at Marvin across the field who was talking to other boys. I had no idea how she knew that, but I trusted her. I nodded as I breathed and entered the school building. I quickly found room 349 and sat down in the very back, knowing the actions of "new-student-in-the-front-of-the-class" drama. I just opened my S.S. notebook and ducked my head down.

"Melissa?" I heard someone murmur with a playful and hopeful smirk. At first, I didn't lift my head up to see who it was. Alexander, Ember, and Sabrine don't have any classes with me, the boys aren't in my grade, and that's not Faye's voice. I lifted my head anyway and was so glad I did.

"Abree!" I laughed, ushering her to sit down next to me as I pulled her into a tight hug. I felt so happy at that moment and all the previous stress and fear floated away from me.

"How are you? What classes are you in?" I squealed, wanting to know it all right away. She laughed and I pulled my schedule out of my binder. She looked it over and gave it back with a tired smile.

"I'm in your Math, Science, S.S and of course recess & lunch with you," Abree giggled as she took my hand in hers. I was about to ask her more questions when the teacher walked in.

"Good morning class. Today I would like to introduce you to a new student. Melissa Logan, would you please stand and come to the front?" the teacher smiled wickedly as he beckoned me forward. I awkwardly stood and slowly walked to the front of the room. I faced him to shake his hand and then faced the crowd of interesting faces.

"I'm Mr. Walter, and can you say 10 things about yourself to the class? Group? Get ready," Mr. Walter said as he sat in his chair. I cleared my throat and smiled my calm smile to the class.

"Well, I'm Melissa Logan," I started, but before anyone else could move or I could say anything, a tomato was thrown at me and blew up in my face, tomato guts dripping down my chin. I decided that all I can do is continue.

"I'm 12," Another tomato.
"I have a boyfriend," A third tomato sliding down my hair.
"I am in 7th grade," Fourth tomato.
"I have two moms," Spitting a fifth tomato out of my mouth.
"I have three brothers," Sixth tomato.
"I play basketball," Tomato guts were now in my socks.

"I like to read," Seventh tomato.
"I hate avocados," Tomato bled through my
top, turning it deep red.
"My dad is a teacher," Ninth tomato.
"I have broken my leg,"

Finally, 5 cherry Slushies were slammed
into my face. I gasped as it slapped my neck, bled
through my jeans & stung my face, but I didn't say
a word. Mr. Walters stood and laughed at me.

"Welcome to Dunwich Academy, Melissa.
Please take a seat," Mr. Walters hissed happily. I
shook my arms and quickly walked to my seat.
Abree looked at me with horror and her note on my
desk told me that every new student gets it and she
got water balloons and a grape Slushie. I sighed
and wrote down the notes on the chalkboard like
everyone else. After a trip to the bathroom,
Spanish, and Math class, it was finally time for
lunch and recess. I walked outside and I let the
wind carry me to the swings. Spending the whole
recess period on the swings was calming, but
isolating. When the lunch bell rang, I grabbed a
salad with fruit, a brownie, and a soda and joined
Marvin, Gale, Alexander, Ember, Sabrine, Faye,
and Abree at a table.

"So, how was your first three classes,
Melissa?" Gale wondered, staring at me curiously
as he stuffed some cheese bread in his mouth. I
sighed and just laughed to myself.

"Pretty good, actually. I was greeted with
tomatoes and a cherry Slushie in S.S., learned
three new words in Spanish, and was the first to
finish a hard equation in Math," I answered, pouring

ranch over my salad. I was about to ask how was the boys' day, but Ember decided it was her turn to talk.

"Marvin? Gale? Can you please leave for just a second? I think they're giving out special pop tarts right now," Ember smirked. The boys beamed at her and hastened in line for pop tarts. Ember turned towards me and gave me her wicked smile, "like I said yesterday, I have more things to tell you. After school, you have to do all of your homework, and then you are free to hang out in the living room, tv room, arcade or the chat area. At 8:30 you go to the dining room to eat dinner and then you have some more free time. Curfew is at 10:30. Got it?" Ember hissed. I nodded and she quickly nodded back. Out of nowhere, she finished her food and dragged Sabrine over to another table with a bunch of other girls. Gale and Marvin were eating pop tarts with their friends, and Faye and Abree left to see other people, so it was just me and Alexander.

"Sorry about all of that. My sister can be a little bit of a diva and jerk sometimes," Alexander shrugged. I spit up my sip of soda and started to laugh into my can. I looked at him and slowly breathed to contain my giggles.

"Wait, wait, wait. Ember is your sister??" I breathed. I laughed in my scarf, and laughed even harder when Alexander laughed with me.

"No, I'm just kidding. Sabrine is my sister. Ember's family have been close friends with our family since we were kids, so we've known each other for a while," Alexander answered, giggling at me. I kept on laughing until suddenly, Alexander grabbed my hand in his. I was in total shock, but let his warm hand warm up mine.

"Alexander, have you always been this sweet?" I sighed, placing my hand over his. He smiled and scooted closer over to me.

"Well, you can call me Alex from now on. By the way, you're about to get Slushied again. Everyone new kid gets Slushied again during lunch," Alex smiled and sighed. I giggled and turned towards the main door. The lunch supervisor, Mr. Walters, Ms. Bea my Spanish teacher, Mr. James my Math teacher, Ms. Caylor my Science teacher, and Mr. Tiger my L.A teacher walked outside and stood in front of me. As the teachers formed a circle, Ms. Bea ushered me to stand in the middle and one by one, each teacher threw in my face a cold Slushie. With orange dripping down my back, red hugging my hair, yellow gripping at my shoes, green bleeding through my shirt and scarf, blue stinging my face, and purple painting my jeans, I smiled and went to go get cleaned up yet again. Marvin came with me and joined me outside for our free period.

"Melissa, I feel like something's bothering you. Want to talk about it?" Marvin asked. I smiled and shrugged. It was Shane. I wasn't ready to tell him, but my 6-year-old bro is definitely ready, I think.

"It happened right before I came here. Jere and I weren't allowed to see each other but this boy set us up so that I would come here. That boy was my brother, my half brother," I confessed. Marvin's face switched right from caring to betrayal. He just sat there and out of nowhere he sprang up from where he sat and ran back inside. I thought about calling him back, but I knew deep down he had every right to run and be mad at me. I spent the rest of my free time staring at the glum sky and then Science and L.A class went by in a haze. As I dragged myself out of L.A class, Mr. Tiger pulled me back and asked me to take a seat. I groaned but sat down and faced him with tiring and frustrating eyes.

"Melissa, I think I see potential in you," Mr. Tiger acknowledged, "I want to see if I'm not just betting on the new girl. You are assigned a project with Simon Reynolds, separate from class. Write a 6 page essay about anything, but it has to be in depth. In case you were wondering, he is in your Spanish class, L.A class, and in your Free Period. You are dismissed," he yawned, shooing me out of the room. I didn't even ask how he knew my schedule but instead ran out of the room and to my locker.

After I finished gathering my homework and slowly locking my locker, a girl stood next to me, grinning so wide that you would've thought she just saw Justin Bieber back in 2011.

"Hello! My name is Chloe and I believe I'm in your S.S., Science, and L.A class?" Chloe chirped. I feel like I have never seen her in my life, but then my light bulb clicked in my mind. *Chloe, the perky girl.* I thought. I nodded and started to walk towards the exit to school.

"Yeah, I remember you. The one who always raises her hand and when you get called you talk nonstop. You're so cheerful," I giggled, sighing to myself.

"Listen, I would love to stay and chat but I have homework and plans. See you tomorrow?" I asked, walking backwards and reaching out behind me to seek out the door. She smiled, nodded, and skipped in the other direction. I breathed and jogged all the way back to the dormitory building. I pulled out my key and was about to unlock the door, when I heard screaming through the door. About to yell for help, I recognized the screaming voice. Ember. I laughed and kept walking down to the dormitory library.

I sat in the corner and started to work on my Science homework. The next few events came all at once, in a blur. Three boys surrounded me, asking me what I was doing. I said Science homework, and then fists and feet were flying. Everything went black moments later.

"Melissa? Melissa, can you hear me?" Alex yelled, but he seemed distant. I fluttered my eyes open and looked at Alex and our room. I knew he wasn't my boyfriend, and I only met him yesterday, but I was so alone that I couldn't help it. My groans reached a fever pitch as I started to cry and sat up as much as I could to get hugged by Alex. I ate some leftover dinner and went to bed.

Friday, April 13, 2018.
6:07 in the morning.

Sitting up in my bed, sprang huge amounts of pain throughout my entire body. Looking over at my bed stand, I found my homework finished and my breakfast waiting, making me grin. I got up and flowed into the silent get ready routine. After settling on dark jeans, "Don't go with the flow" tank top and a messy bun, I mouthed a thank you to Alex and quickly walked out the door.

After a slow S.S. class, I remembered that Simon was in my next class. Searching the room as I walked into Spanish, a group of boys were smirking and pointing at me. At first I didn't care, but when one of them turned around to face me, my blood and anger quickly boiled up. In a swift move I was able to pull him into the hallway. I stared at him as I grabbed his jacket and pulled him closer to my face.

"If you bring your fists or your feet near my body again, one of them is coming off. Got it?" I hissed. The boy showed a moment of fear, but shyly shrugged me off.

"My name is Sage. You are?" Sage wondered, offering me his hand. I smirked and smacked it. I turned around and walked into the classroom, shouting my name behind me. Ms. Bea soon called class to start and had us all seated to call attendance. Somewhere in the attendance call, Simon's name was called and I heard an answer. I turned my head towards the voice and saw a slim boy with super gelled hair. I smirked as I scribbled a note to him and passed it to him.

Simon,
Hello. I'm Melissa. I'm in your Spanish class, L.A class, and we have free period together? Mr. Tiger assigned us a project to work on, a 6 page essay on something deep. When should we start?

Melissa

 I slipped it on his desk and continued my activity with my group. Just a few minutes later, a note flew by me and I caught it as I read it.

Melissa,
Why not? Free period, the library at school. See you then.

Simon

 I sighed and some of my stress was lifted off of my shoulders. Not only did I start my project, but that means that I won't have to spend my free period alone. Marvin and Simon are the only ones that I know that are in my free period, so. I went to Math and got 22/44 correct on a speed test. It feels wrong, not getting them all right, not being in my dad's class. I miss him. Definitely prefer him over Mr. James over here.

"Melissa! Over here!" Abree yelled over the crowd during lunch, calling me over. I sat down with my lunch and sighed. I'm so glad the girls are here with me, because right now I'm on the edge of surviving.

"How are you?" Faye asked. I smiled and started to pick through my salad.

"I'm doing fine. I got beat up yesterday though, and I have to do this stupid project that Mr. Tiger assigned me and this Simon. Honestly, I need a girls night right now," I laughed, remembering the girl nights that Teresa held for me and the girls every few weekends.

"Maybe you can come sleepover with us tonight! Our second and third person hasn't come yet, so there's an empty bed for you. We can watch movies and stay up late since it's a Friday and there's no school tomorrow," Abree exclaimed. I shrugged in possible agreement and we talked about all the junk food we're going to eat.

You would think that I would know when someone is coming up behind me, since that has happened many times before. But when Simon grabbed me by the shoulder and twisted me towards him, I was in total shock and terrified.

"Ready to work?" He muttered, looking at me straight in the eye. I had no idea what he was talking about, but then my mind brought me back to the passing of notes scenario.

"Yes, I'm ready to work. Can you meet me at our place please? It's not even free period yet," I asked sternly. Simon groaned but let go of me and walked away. I suddenly heard giggling behind and turned back around to see Abree and Faye giggling in their shawls.

"What?" I asked, suddenly very worried. Abree pulled her shawl down and gently grabbed me by the arm.

"Simon Reynolds, huh? We've known him for a while and that was definitely his flirting side. He likes you!" Abree exclaims. I laugh and shake my hand as I grab another bite of my yogurt.

"First of all, we just met earlier in Spanish class only because Mr. Tiger assigned us a project. Second of all, he does not like me," I muttered. Faye shook her head and offered me a cookie.

"Trust me, that was his flirting side. I used to date him," Faye confessed, breathing in deep, "we dated for a week and then we broke up. I'm dating Sage now. Know him?" Faye asked. I gasped and dropped my spoon on my tray. I wasn't mad at Faye, but really wondered if she knew who he really was.

"Well, I have Sage in my Spanish and Math classes. Also, Sage and his crew were the ones who beat me up yesterday in the library," I sighed, holding Faye's hand tight.

"But, I talked to him during Spanish and I think he is a great guy. Even if Simon did like me, I still have a boyfriend. See you guys later," I finished as the bell rang.

Simon was waiting for me in the corner of the library when I got there. I sat down and we just stared at each other for a moment. Out of nowhere, Simon jumped into the project and was ready to go.

"So, what do you want this 6 page essay to be about?" Simon asked as he sat down across from me with maybe 12 pages in one hand and four pencils. I rest my head on my hands and started to think. *What should we right about?*

"Well, I've heard that you're parents are divorced and your dad isn't your birth dad," I whispered, "I have the same situation. Except it's my mom that isn't my birth mom and my parents aren't divorced, there just not seeing each other right now. Want to write about that, our experiences?" I asked. Simon looked into my eyes, and smiled. I smiled back and we started writing. When the school bell rang and I walked out of there, there was something that I never thought I would say to Simon, thanks.

"Melissa! What are you doing?" Alex asked me later when I walked in and started to pack some of my stuff. I smiled and rested on my bed.

"It's Friday night and my girls are hosting a girls night at their place, a sleepover," I mumbled, rubbing my head with my hands. Alex grinned and helped me pack my stuff. I smiled and finally stood up to leave. I walked for what seems forever trying to find Faye and Abree's place, and was about to give up when I heard my name. Called out by a very familiar voice. I turn around and at the end of the hall stands Jere, with a backpack, his new keys and school supplies. I dropped my stuff, all of it clattering to the floor.

"Jere?" I whispered, on the verge of tears. My legs were exploding with adrenaline but for some reason, I don't run towards him. *Was this an illusion? Is someone tricking me?*

"Melissa," Jere whispered, a tired smile quickly appearing on his face. At that very moment, I knew it was true. I knew that he is here. My engines start up and I start sprinting towards him. Jere drops all of his stuff and has his arms open wide when I get there. I run into them and once I feel Jere's arms wrap around me, I start crying.

"I haven't realized until now how much I missed you," I sobbed, continuing to cry in his arms as Jere holds onto me tighter.

"Why didn't you realized you missed me so much until now?" Jere asks calmly, while holding back tears. I lift my hand and let out a tired laugh as I wipe the tears sliding down my face.

"Well, when I got here, I lost all hope. When I saw my brothers though, I felt so much better. But realizing where I am gave me no hope for coming back home, to you, so I decided to let you go and pretend it didn't hurt me. Now I realize that I was hiding a lot of hurt," I smile. Jere smiled too and lifted me into the air, making me crack up.

"Now, can you tell me what to do next since I'm new here?" Jere asked. I grab my stuff and gently push him to show him where his room is, telling him what to do after that.

"So, I was supposed to have a girls night with Faye and Abree tonight," I sighed as I sat down on the bed next to his. No one else was in his room, giving the space all to himself (lucky).

"I would love to hang out with you more, but my roommates are expecting me," I finished slowly, hoping he wouldn't be mad. But Jere just nodded. I kissed him on the cheek and walked out the door, grinning. Jere has given me some sort of superpower, now that he's here with me. I unlocked Faye's and Abree's door, got in my pjs and got in bed without making a sound. I had wonderful dreams that night, but those dreams were destroyed when the Voice decided to pay a visit.

Ok, Melissa. You've had all your fun. Time to get serious. If you don't start trying to stop me, people are getting hurt. Permanently. Sweet dreams.

Saturday, April 14, 2018.
7:30 in the morning.

I find it very interesting that I wake up and head back to my dorm at 7:30 in the morning on a **Saturday,** and I find work waiting for me on my desk. I sit on my bed and find a note folded on my bed stand. It's not crumpled, so it wasn't from Alex. It wasn't smothered in hearts, so it wasn't Sabrine. It didn't have words teasing me and my name all over it, so it wasn't from Ember. As I pull on my light jeans and a snug gray N.Y. sweatshirt, I saw that the note was from Simon.

Melissa,

Great idea for the project! Want to work on it more today? It's ok if you don't want to. Just come to the library, like last time.

Simon

I smiled as I grabbed my notebook and left the dorm. I passed Jere in the hallway and told him I'll meet him at lunch. I arrive at the library and Simon waves me over so we can get to work. But instead of working, he leans in and almost kisses me, which I was **not** ready for.

"Simon! Are you crazy?! I have a boyfriend you know. I think we should just get this assignment done, ok?" I sternly yell as I quickly back up. Simon sits back down, but for some reason still has a smirk on his face.

"But your boyfriend isn't here, right?" Simon adds as he leans back in. I laugh and stop him firmly with my hand. I sit him back down and grip his shoulder.

"Well, news flash. My boyfriend arrived late after school yesterday. I really, truly like you Simon, but I think it's better anyway that we're friends. See you Monday, ok?" replied, letting go as I stood up. Simon nodded and I breathed as I tried to find Chloe. Surprisingly, she was at the other side of the library. I tapped her shoulder and once she saw me, all the fun and the cheerful side of her switched right on.

"Wassup?" Chloe asks. I shrug and leaned against the bookshelf.

"My boyfriend just came yesterday and one of my brothers hate me and Simon tried to kiss me and-" I quickly confessed as my heart started to hasten and my hands started to shake.

"Woah, woah honey. First of all, calm yourself down! Second, it seems like Envy Ember hasn't shown you one of the best things about this place. Come on!" Chloe smiles, pulling me out of the library and across the street of the school. After 10 minutes of passcodes, secret doors, and turning off the lights, we walked into something so breathtaking, I almost wanted to stay there forever.

It was huge room that glowed with writing and drawing, covering the walls. They all sparked and enlightened me inside. I let go of Chloe's hand and brushed my hand over the ideas and inspiration that stuck to the walls. I smiled and suddenly all of me let go. Even when Jere came, I still felt unsafe and uptight. In this place, I feel like the last few weeks had never happened and I can be Melissa, the teenager with a dad, mom, and two brothers. I looked down and laughed.

The floor was camouflaged with pictures. Pictures of everyone. I knelt down and looked at all of my new friends and us, smiling and laughing. Chloe snuck up behind me and rested her head on my shoulder.

"This is our room. Whenever we feel like giving up, we come here. No parties, just a place to bring back our hope. These," Chloe smiled, tracing over all the pictures plastered to the ground, "these are pictures of us when we were happy, before all of this. It gives us a reminder and comfort that at one point in our lives, we were happy. We all hope that we will be happy again," Chloe sighed, holding my hand in hers. I smiled, pulled out a picture of Jere and I at the picnic before he left for Georgia, and glued it on the ground.

Suddenly, I remembered what the Voice told me last night. I jumped up and started to lead us to the door.

"I'm so sorry that I can't hang out with you longer, but I need to find my boyfriend and my friends. See you at later though!" I requested as I ran out the door and back to the dormitory building. I gathered Faye, Abree, and Jere outside and started to break things down.

"Ok. The Voice told me last night that if I, we didn't start to figure things out, someone will get seriously hurt. So let's figure all of this out," I started, stammering through my sentences and folding my hands multiple times. Jere took my hands and I felt safe to stop shaking.

"Can I just ask why the "Death Call" kidnaps us and sends us to a not so bad place? It's actually kinda cool here," Faye mentioned. I nodded and thought about that for a second. *Why would the Death Call send us to an awesome place??*

"Also, why are kids from other schools here? I thought the "Death Call" did one curse at a time. Is that theory no longer true?" Jere added. I suddenly realized that if we wanted to get any more information on the school and/or the dormitories, we need to get close to the person that runs this place. The "Death Call" manager. I stood up and beckoned everyone to follow me back to my room to find the person I sadly need, Ember.

"What do you need Melissa?" Ember smirked as she put down her magazine and stood to stare at me. I smirked back at her and sat on my bed while everyone else waited outside.

"Do you know who runs this whole place? Or like, where they could be?" I asked, carefully picking my words, knowing how tight Ember can get.

"Why?" Ember muttered, holding her magazine close, but eyeing me carefully.

"Well, I had a personal question about something," I answered, twisting my fingers around my scarf, hoping she'd buy it.

"School building. Two rooms to the right of Mr. Tiger's. Have fun," Ember retorted. I grinned, jumped up and sprinted out with my friends back to the school. We slowly crept past Mr. Tiger's room, and soon enough, we were in front of the principal's office. I gripped the door handle and pushed it open, immediately thinking that closing the door was plan B.

"Ms. Genie!" I quietly yelled. Ms. Genie ushered us to sit down, and surprisingly there were 4 seats waiting for us. After a moment of consideration, we decided to sit.

"Please, Melissa. Call me mom!" Ms. Genie exclaimed, "So, what do you think of the place? Ask me some questions. Let's hang out," Ms. Genie asked.

"I'm asking you two questions, and I'm out. Comprende?" I said sternly. Mrs. Genie slowly nodded, "Number 1, why are you keeping us here when it's a wonderful place? Number 2, where are **all** of my brothers?" I ended with a snarl.

"1, you're going to have to figure that one yourself. 2, Marvin and Gale are room R15. Shane, R23," Ms. Genie smirked back. I smiled greedily and raced out of the room, not waiting for anyone to follow me. I slowed down to room R23 and banged on the door. Shane opened the door and I took no hesitation to punch him straight in the face. Blood spluttered from his nose and his teeth shined red. Before he could do anything back, I kicked him in the stomach and ran.

Sunday, April 15, 2018.
2:30 in the morning.

Out of nowhere, rough hands covered my mouth and were wrapped around my body. I screamed and yanked, trying to at least loosen their grip on me. I screamed for Jere, Alex, Sabrine, anyone. Hot tears dripped down to my mouth and they tasted bitter. Suddenly, the people stopped. I breathed a relief, but held it right back in when those rough hands let go of me. I screamed as my body banged against the ground and extreme amounts of pain surrounded me. I gasped and tried to breathe as my conscious quickly ran away from me. But just before I closed my eyes, I saw Ms. Genie in the distance. She was running towards me, yelling my name.

Sunday, April 15, 2018.
9:00 in the morning.

I woke up in tears and sweat all over my pajama shirt. I looked over to my left and saw Ms. Genie stared at me with big worried eyes. I grimaced and tried to sit up. Ms. Genie immediately stopped me and gave me what seemed like medicine, but tasted like jalapenos dipped in blue cheese. I roughly swallowed and while pushing her away, I carefully sat up. I sighed and as by body relaxed and all my muscles got very tense. I grimaced and looked at Ms. Genie with curiosity. She lightly smiled back and slowly reached out to my hands. I stiffened when she held them but accepted, too tired to argue.

"I'm so sorry Melissa. The people that attacked you were your brothers, all three of them. They looked like they were going to drop you in the lake near school, but I found you just in time. They dropped you on the ground and ran when I caught them. Sabrine, one of the girls you share a dorm with? She dropped some clothes off when she heard from Alexander, your other roommate," Ms. Genie sighed. As my body adjusted to the blast of pain in every step I took, I slowly pulled on turquoise jeans and I let my curled brown locks rolled down in every which way, only controlled by a light blue bow.

I didn't say goodbye to Ms. Genie. Once she left for her "work", I left a note saying thanks and limped back over to my room. No one was in there when I got there, so I decided to have a relax day by myself. I was asleep when the door was knocked on and my eyes fluttered open. I was upset and ungrateful for my life in the moment, but when I opened the door, I felt so lucky. Standing outside my door was my Marvin and Gale. Instead of being mad at them, I started to cry and we all ended up sinking to the floor, crying and holding each other. Jere sent the three of us dinner later so that we didn't have to go to the dining room.

Now it was late and everyone was asleep except Alexander and me. We talked and I felt really good talking to him about things that I have had trouble thinking about myself.

"So, there's an assembly tomorrow, replacing our Period 1. You ready for your first one?" Alex asked quietly, staring longingly in my eyes. He knows I have a boyfriend, they met earlier, but he always knew how to be a romantic. Also, I knew he still had feelings for me, no matter what. I'm glad he knew where the line stood, unlike Simon.

"Yeah, I guess. As ready as I'll ever be. We should probably get to bed," I yawned, hugging him tightly before I lightly jumped into my bed. Alex leaned in and hugged me back before he walked over to his bed as well. I watched him from where I was from that moment on, mesmerized by the everlasting memory of his smile.

Monday, April 16, 2018.
6:04 in the morning.

"Melissa, wake up! Wake up! I chose some options for you to wear to your first assembly! You must be so excited! Come on, get up!" Sabrine cheered as she shook me awake. I jumped up in shock and groaned as morning rose up inside of my still asleep body.

There was an assortment of my hats, shoes, shirts, jeans, skirts and scarfs set up like a store on top of my dresser. I smiled at Sabrine's taste of clothing as I picked up a flowered **Word** shirt, white jeans and glitter converses. Sabrine grabbed my hand and quickly lead me out the door, out of the building and into the auditorium at school.

The room was crammed with chairs, teachers, and of course students. For some personally stupid reason, every seat had a name on it for a student. Sabrine let me go with a hug to go find her seat, so I went to find mine.

I ended up being almost smack dab in the middle of the place, in between Alex and Chloe. I was about to ask what exactly happens during an assembly when the crowd's attention transferred from chatting to staring at Mrs. Genie.

"Good morning students. I have some announcements, and then the rest of the assembly will commence. First of all, the teachers and I have decided to have some more trust in you. When you get back to your dorms, you will find your phones from back home and the rules. We hope you can respect these like you do us. Lastly, there will be no student going near the lake until further notice," Ms. Genie reported sweetly, "Thank you, and on to awards and special events. Can we please have Melissa Logan come up?" Ms. Genie, looking down to me.

I shrugged, slowly stood up and walked to the front of the cluster of students of teachers. I looked to Ms. Genie and she smiled back.

"We just wanted to say how happy we are that you are here with us. To show how much we care, we give you these flowers. Enjoy," Ms. Genie said proudly as she handed me a lovely bouquet of white and red roses. I laughed and waved proudly at my new posse. The crowd cheered and for a moment there was happiness.

"Sage, go!" Someone called out in the group of students. There was a second of murmured confusion, including myself. All of a sudden, cold, hard shards of flavored ice connected with my head. I screamed in shock as the huge bowl of slush streamed down my body and hugged my skin. Out of nowhere, Sage and Simon came to the front where I stood, holding more buckets.

"Welcome again, Melissa!" Simon yelled loud enough for everyone to hear him as he and Sage dumped two more freezing Slushies unto me. I screamed again and started crying as the multiple dye colors stung my eyes. All at once, people started to laugh and point kinda behind me and at me. I slowly turned around and started to full-out sob. On the projector in the auditorium was a picture of me with red eyes and a devil's staff. Written in pitch black were the words:

MS. GENIE'S DAUGHTER... THE SLUT IS HERE!!!!!

I held my flowers tightly as my throat grew tight and an imaginary bus hit me in slow motion. I ran off, into the dark of the room, where no one can find me. I went off to clean myself up and walked near the lake. No one was there, so I sat down and cried all of my pain away. I was hurt by so many things in the past and now, so I tucked them inside me since everyone expected me to be tough. Now that all of this has happened, my flood gate has been broken and all of these feelings came out at once. The wind blew strongly towards me and whipped my hair and a pieces of paper all over the place. I picked a piece of paper up and was about to recycle it, but then read part of what was on it. I gasped and ran back to my dorm with the paper. I locked the door behind me and gripped nervously at my recently returned phone when I fully read the entire paper.

...Some students have the inner power over certain situations and can power the Weapon. These students, like Melissa Logan, Jeremiah Baldwin and their friends, are the key to all of the power. If we can get all of them and get their power, the Weapon and everything will fall in place. We also need to be careful about <u>after</u> we take their power. When their power is taken away from them, they are weak, but their other special senses can become stronger. We have to make sure that they don't find out about their other special senses, meaning that they can not go anywhere near the lake! If they do, the whole plan can fall apart...

I threw down the paper and disappeared in tears and worry. A knock on the door came and I opened up the door to see Jere standing there. I started to cry even harder and stumbled into his arms. I held him tightly and let all of myself let go into him. I let it all go until tiredness caught up to me and I drifted off to sleep.

Tuesday, April 17, 2018.
6:05 in the morning.

"Melissa, wake up! It's time to get ready for school," Jere whispered in my ear. I groaned and slowly sat up. I opened my eyes and shook in shock as I fully woke up in a bed next to Jere, in Jere's room. *I slept in Jere's room last night. Why?* I laid on my back and stared at him with curious eyes.

"What happened?" I slurred, "What happened after you met me at my room?"

"Well, I took you to my room to rest so that you wouldn't be bothered by your roommates, told your teachers that you would missing your classes because of the incident, and then I came back for you after school. You were asleep the whole time," Jere sighed as he grabbed a stack of clothes and tossed them to me.

"I told Sabrine about you in Free Period and she gave me your clothes and wanted me to tell you that she'll give your backpack to Abree to give to you," Jere sighed as he went to the bathroom to get changed. I nodded and started to get ready as well. I smirked as I picked through my clothes. I continued to love Sabrine's taste as I pulled on dark jeans, a pale pink top, and braided my hair into a neat fishtail braid. I walked out the door with Jere and prepared for another day.

"Thanks," I muttered as Abree quietly tossed me my backpack during roll call. I found my homework and as I set my backpack down, I grimaced at the graffiti on my desk. **Miss Slushie Slut** was plastered all over and it screamed out to me. I washed it off with wipes and tried my very hardest to survive the day. To everyone else, I was worried about Science Class after Free Period. On the inside, I was freakin' horrified about Spanish class. Sage and Simon are both in that class with me and I'm pretty sure that my tough self can't handle them this time.

Luckily, I didn't experience anything during passing period (although that's surprising), but my Spanish terror started right when I walked in the room. My desk and chair was covered in bright red Slushie. In what smelled like Coca Cola Slushie were the words, **Can you teach us how to be a slut, Ms. Slushie Slut??** I sadly smirked and started to wipe it off my desk and chair. I sat down and stress was lifted off my shoulders when I saw that Simon and Sage weren't in class at all.

I walked in line for lunch later and was surprised by the fact that a Slushie or any other food/drink object hasn't been thrown at me yet. The lunch lady tells me that I have a special lunch ordered for me and I walk over to the ordered area to get my lunch. What gets handed to me, however, is a gallon of lemonade Slushie and later a text from Simon saying, **When life gives you sluts, you make Slushie sluts! Enjoy your lunch.** *How did Simon get my number?* I thought as I sit down and Jere sits down as well, trying his hardest not to laugh at me. I admit that it's a little bit funny, but having my boyfriend laugh at me is just cruel. I push him and at the last second pull him close again.

'It's funny, but it's not funny for you to laugh," I giggle, smuggling in a quick kiss. He smiled, grabbed two big spoons, and we dug in. After we finished, I decided it was time to talk about the paper.

"Jere, can I talk to you?" I whispered as I pulled him in a shaded area. Jere nodded and held my hands in his, "When I ran from the assembly, I found this piece of paper by the lake. It said something about this Weapon that will finish this plan. The "Death Call" brought all of these kids here because they are the power source. The "Death Call" is thinking about sending all of the kids home because it realizes that me, you, and all of our friends can give a lot more power to the main source than anyone else. We're probably going to be the source that destroys the school. We need to do something," I whispered urgently to him. Jere looked really disturbed by this information, but nodded and told me to meet him at the library after school with everyone else. Then he ran off as the bell rang, leaving me to fight for myself. I sent everyone a text explaining the plan before rushing off to Free Period.

"Melissa, can you come here please?" Mr. Tiger asks as I begin to leave L.A class. I nodded and sat back down at the front desk.

"Melissa, I would first like to say how sorry I am for the incident at the assembly yesterday. You don't have to do the make up work from yesterday," Mr. Tiger explained nervously, "but about the paper that I assigned you and Simon. Simon wants to do this paper separately in a competition between the two of you. I'm the judge and the loser has to admit that they are a Slushie Slut? He says that if you agree to this, he won't steal your paper idea. I'm sorry," Mr. Tiger stammered as he tried to hold himself together. I nodded him off in agreement and quickly left the room.

A few moments later, I rushed to join Abree, Faye, and Jere in the library. There were at a deserted area in the far corner and I slammed the paper on the table. The girls read it and looked up at me in complete concern and fear. I slightly nodded and sat down with the rest of them.

"Right after my L.A class, I took the liberty to go to Ms. Genie's office and eavesdrop on her recent conversation. She was talking to this adult male voice and, they discussed everything on the paper. It's all true, they are sending the rest of the kids back in 4 days and our friends will be here in 5 days. We don't have a lot of time to do whatever we're going to do," I inquired. The rest nodded and sat in a moment of silence.

"We have to figure out what to do, but it's not like there's a lot of things to do anyway. Even if there was, it's not like we can do it 4 days," Abree sighed, messing with her intense rings.

"I agree with Abree. There's not a lot of things we can do in 4 days. I think the only thing we can do right now is to be cautious and warn everybody back home," Jere muttered. I smiled and suddenly knew exactly what to do.

"I'll take care of the warning," I answered a little too loudly, "don't worry about it. I got this under control," I said proudly as I stood up and left them to talk.

"Simon! Hey Simon, open up!" I yelled as I banged on Simon's door later on the way to dinner. The door opened and Simon's frown switched automatically to a huge grin. He stepped out of the hallway and quietly closed the door behind him, keeping all eyes on me.

"I just wanted to let you know that I can't wait to destroy you at the writing competition. Let's see if it takes you the whole 2 weeks we have to realize that you don't even need to try. I'm gonna win," I smirked at him. Simon laughed and stared right back at me.

"You're right, I don't need to try. Do you think it's going to take you 2 weeks or 2 years to write the thing?" Simon hollered as he softly pushed me and walked away. I laughed as well as I went to tell Mr. Tiger that Simon and I will have our papers ready in 3 days, not 2 weeks.

Wednesday, April 18, 2018.
7:30 in the morning.
3 days until the separation.

I strutted down the hallway in my light blue collar shirt, hot pink jeans, and cute white pumps, excited for the unexpected events of today to occur. Jere came up behind me and laced my hand in his, and we were suddenly the couple of the hall. I smiled as I slowly let go of his hand and kissed him goodbye as I started out my day.

"Melissa, can I talk to you?" I heard someone mumble to me as I worked on my paper during Free Period in the library. I turned around and looked to find Sage standing behind of me. I scoffed at him and turned back to my paper.

"What do you want, jerk?" I snapped intensely as I dug my pencil into my paper.

"I just wanted to say how sorry I am about the incident. I was flirting and-" Sage started to explain, but I became so furious that I stood up and slapped him across the face.

"You think beating the crap out of me in the library, dumping pounds of Slushie on me, calling me 'Miss Slushie Slut', and playing along in giving me a gallon of Slushie for lunch is flirting!?" I quietly yelled at him.

"I don't know how you people flirt back at your school, but at my school, that's called bullying. Leave me alone, Sage," I muttered as I quickly grabbed my stuff and left the library.

Later, I got back to my room to see only Alex there, playing his guitar on the edge of his bed. I smiled and sat down next to him to hear him play. When he finished he turned towards me and grinned, softly bumping his hand into mine.

"That's called "Everlasting Friendships", and I wrote that because I think that's what we are, right?" Alex recalled as I bumped my hand back.

"Yes, we are, we will always be," I sighed, "Alex, can you keep a secret for me?" I asked softly, resting my head on his shoulder. Alex nodded and I felt his ear brush across my head.

"Alex, this secret is a little hard to say. Ms. Genie is going to send all of us back home in three days. She's not going to send Jere, Abree, Faye, or myself back though," I mumbled. I sat up and looked at his confused face, making tears appear in my eyes.

"Hey, it's going to be ok. We will see each other again, as best friends. I will give you my number (for friend reasons only), but I need you to do me a favor," I said softly, "When you get home, can you go to Foxborough Elementary & Middle School and tell Lacey, Lucy, Kennedy, Amber, Belle, Samira, Rosemary, Trent, and Gavin that we will see each other soon. They'll know what you mean. Can you do that for me?" I asked. Alex lifted his head and nodded as more tears sprinkled down his cheeks. I wrote down my number and slipped it into his hand.

"Can I ask why you don't call Ms. Genie your mom?" Alex questioned. I laughed quietly and covered my face with my hands.

"I don't call her mom because I don't think of her as my mom. She abandoned me and my dad a week after I was born. Teresa, my mom, she found us and took care of us. She married my dad when I was 10 months old and then later had Gale and Marvin. Also, Ms. Genie is the principal at Foxborough back home. When I first went to there for Kindergarten, I had my dad as a math teacher. Over my 7 years of being at that school, neither decided to tell me. I actually just found out right before I came here so," I answered, standing up and walking to the door. I laughed at Alex's dumbfounded face as I beckoned him to come to dinner with me. We sat with Marvin, Gale, Jere, Abree, Faye, and Barrett also came to join us.

"I already told them about what's going to happen. I assume Alex knows?" Jere inquired as he dug into his mashed potatoes. Alex nodded and I reached out to grab Marvin and Gale's hands.

"I can't leave you, Melissa. I won't leave you, especially with Ms. Genie," Marvin whimpered, squeezing my hand.

"I'll be fine. I'll come for you, both of you soon enough. Your job is to go straight to dad and mom and tell them that I'll be ok. Will you do that for me?" I plead. After a moment, they nodded and we launched back into our lovely friend dinner. I left a few minutes early and went back to the dorms to work on my paper. I fell asleep writing these few words, these few words that were swirling inside my head.

Families are like branches on a tree. We grow in different directions, yet our roots remain as one.

Thursday, April 19, 2018.
6:30 in the morning.
2 days until the separation.

The alarm on my phone shook my soundless body awake. I quickly sat up in bed and looked around the room. It looked like Ember just left the room and the room smelled strongly of mint and strawberries. I stood to find that Sabrine has chosen my outfit for today, again. Sabrine decided on a dark blue and white tank top, dark jeans, and left a text saying that I should let my curls out. I smiled and on the way to S.S. class, the loving Chloe joined me.

"Sage wants to know what you like to do after school hours. Why is he asking you that when he has a girlfriend?" Chloe asked curiously as we sat down and started on our Do Now.

"He wants to go out with me. But there are 3 reasons why I would never. One, he's a jerk. Two, he's dating Faye, my friend. Three, I'm seeing someone. I'm breaking the news to Faye and Sage during lunch," I replied.

"Melissa! I got you something! I heard you were getting a gallon of grape Slushie for lunch today so I got something special for you," Faye yelling as she ran into me at the snack court. She breathed a smile and gave me a huge McDonald's bag. I laughed and hugged her close as we found a seat.

"Thank you. There's actually, something I need to tell you. Sage was flirting with me in the library yesterday and asked me out. I know that he's leaving in two days, but please dump him. You deserve better," I pleaded as I picked at my BBQ with my chicken. At first, I could tell that she was considering this decision, but I could tell she knew what the right choice was.

"Hey babe, want to go for gelato before lunch ends?" Sage called from across the court. Faye slightly smiled and walked real close to him.

"I'm sorry Sage, did you mean to say that to me or Melissa? What we have, it's over jerk," Faye spat at him. Sage glared back at her but backed off in disgust and walked back across the court. The bell rang and I proudly waved her off to class as I walked to the library. Surprisingly, Ms. Genie was waiting for me.

"What do you want?" I snapped at her as I sat down.

"I just wanted to check on you. I know that what Simon, Sage, and a couple of other kids did was awful. I'm sorry that-" Ms. Genie explained but I didn't want to hear any more of it.

"You know what? It's fine. Thank you for saying I'm sorry **three days** after it actually happened. Now if you excuse me, I'm going to hang out with people that actually care about 'Miss Slushie Slut,'" I said sternly, packing up my stuff and quickly skipping off and out of the library and to the secret place that Sabrine showed me. I stayed there the rest of the period and for a moment, I imagined a world like this room, where life was simple and full of magic. I liked that life. After a few minutes of believing that I was in that life for real, I got interrupted by a text that sadly brought me back to reality.

Melissa,
Ms. Genie wants you, me, Faye, and Abree in her office in 5 minutes. See u there.

Love ya ❤❤
Jere

I sighed as I stood up and escorted myself up to Ms. Genie's office. I walked in sat down next to Jere, Abree, and Faye and got my getaway feet ready.

"We are going to be making a few changes around here. Saturday, April 21, you four will be transferring to new rooms and new lockers. Melissa, your new room will be R1 and your new locker will be Locker 1. Jeremiah, your new room is also R1 and you're Locker 2. Faye, R2 and Locker 3. Abree, also R2 and Locker 4. Thank you," Ms. Genie requested. We all nodded and hurried out of the room and straight to our classes.

"I bet you that whole new rooms and lockers thing had something to do with all of the kids leaving and us staying. Like putting the 13 of us together to keep an eye on us or something," Abree muttered as we relaxed in the chat room. I just shrugged and wrapped my hand into Jere's.

"I don't think it's that bad, for now. We all get new rooms with our friends. I get to be with my Jere, so for me I'm good," I smiled as I picked with my shirt with one hand while squeezing Jere's hand with the other. Faye laughed and pushed Abree off of the picnic table. I laughed as well and beckoned everyone in so they can hear me.

"I can't wait for tomorrow. You know that paper that Simon and I are competing for? Simon thinks that it's due in 2 weeks. But I told Mr. Tiger that it's due tomorrow. I'll win and Simon will have to admit that he's a Slushie Slut!" I giggled. The rest of them laughed and we high-fived each other.

"Hey, Simon! Wait up!" I yell as I race Simon out of the cafeteria later. Simon ignored me all the way to the dorm rooms until I rammed into him. He turned and glared at me.

"What do you need?" Simon snarled at me. I was taken aback by his assumption that I _needed_ **his** help, but smiled back at him like nothing fazed me.

"I don't **_need_** anything from you, Simon. I just wanted to make sure you get some good sleep tonight and that you have the best dream you've got," I grinned. Simon looked puzzled for a second but turned right back to his serious, straight face.

"Why would I need to do that?" Simon asked curiously. I smiled and started to walk down the hallway, Simon lurking behind me.

"I just think you'll need it for what's coming for you tomorrow," I sighed. I turned a corner and slowly pulled out my key as I started to head towards my dorm.

"What? What's going to happen tomorrow?" Simon questioned anxiously as he jogged to catch up to me. I unlocked my door and creeped behind the tight squeeze i made for myself.

"Let's just say that you're gonna get what's coming to you. Have a great rest of your night!" I grinned. I slammed the door and fell on my bed in laughter.

Friday, April 20, 2018.
6:00 sharp in the morning.

I woke up right at 6:00 and jumped out of bed with a jump in my step. I shook Alex, Sabrine, and surprisingly Ember up, put some music on to get ready for the day; our last day together. While the sleepy eyes faded away, I ran to my dresser and picked out a pink top, a city skirt, black heels, and lightly curled my hair at the tips. I grabbed my paper and before Ember could yell at me, Alex tell me goodbye, or Sabrine comment on my outfit, I raced out of the room and down to my classes.

After S.S. and Spanish, I met up with Jere and he kindly walked me down the hallway, gripping my hand so that I don't float into the sky.

"What is up with you? I haven't seen you this happy in a long time," Jere nervously smiled at me as we walked into Math class and sat down.

"I don't know. This is our last day having to see all of these people and Simon is going to be pissed. I will miss Alex, Chloe, Sabrine, those people though," I whispered. Jere laughed and kissed me on the cheek. I smiled back but then frowned. *This is the last day I'll see them, because they get to go back home. I don't, we don't.* I thought. I pushed the thought out of my mind and focused on the math problem in front of me.

"Melissa and Simon, stay for a minute please," Mr. Tiger said as the rest of the class was dismissed. Chloe mouthed a "good luck" and rushed out of the room. I smiled, reached for my paper and slowly walked to the front of the room. I had to push down all of my laughter when I saw Simon's confused face as he walked up with me.

"What is this about, Mr. Tiger?" Simon questioned. I pulled up a chair, Simon did so as well, and we sat down while Mr. Tiger sat in thought.

"Well, today is the due date for those papers. So, hand them over so I can quickly read them and then we can all go," Mr. Tiger said stiffly. I quickly handed mine over and intensely watched him as he read. Just because I knew I was going to win doesn't mean I don't get to try, right?

"Excellent job, Melissa! I knew you had it in you. I just love your subject that you wrote about. Now, Simon? Where's your paper?" Mr. Tiger asked, leaning towards Simon. Simon sat in total shock. I snorted a laugh as he processed what was going on.

"I-I-I don't have my paper finished," Simon stuttered as he messed with is vintage tie. Mr. Tiger leaned back in his chair in anger, but then folded his arms and looked at both of us.

"Well, since you didn't finish your paper, you are disqualified. Meaning that Melissa won the contest and you have to admit you're a Slushie Slut," Mr. Tiger answered. Simon's face turned white and I suddenly couldn't help it. I burst in laughter and patted Simon's back.

"Come on, say it! That was the deal, Simon," I beamed. Simon face went from white to red in 10 seconds and his palms turned into fists. He breathed and slowly turned towards me.

"I… am…. a… Slushie…. Slut," Simon spat out. I laughed, grabbed my stuff and walked out of the room. Right before I walked out, I turned to look at Simon.

"See? You did what you did and it came back to bite you. Have a great rest of your day!" I smiled as I skipped down to my locker and then down to Faye and Abree's room, where everyone was waiting. I knocked on the door and once I saw their faces, I burst into laughter all over again. We collapsed on the floor and talked about our last day. After a while, we went to dinner and Ember, Sabrine, Alex, Marvin, Gale, Faye, Abree, Jere, and I all sat down together.

"Oh, Melissa. Just when I thought you were finally mature, you went back down to immature just then," Ember smirked as she picked at her mashed potatoes and flicked a piece at me. I wiped it off my cheek and flipped my asparagus right back at her.

"I never thought I'd say this but I'm really going to miss you," I smirked. Ember grinned and finally decided to eat her food instead of throwing it. I smiled and tapped on Jere's shoulder as I sipped on some Coca Cola. Jere looked at me and I pulled him over to the corner.

"Hey," I said quietly, "I want you to know for sure that Alex likes me. We discussed it and he knows that we can just be friends. But he's my friend and it's our last night with each other and I-" I said quickly but stopped when Jere grabbed my hands and held them close.

"You want to give him a special night, like a kiss, so he can get the feelings out of his mind and all of that and you can say goodbye. That's fine. I trust you and Alex. You do what you think is right," Jere said, tucking a strand of hair behind my ear. I kissed him as a thank you and we walked back to the table. Alex and I stayed at the table as everyone left and finally it was time to go back to the dorms. Sabrine and Ember were already asleep, so we wrapped ourselves in our blankets and snuggled on the floor.

"You know, if I ever see you again, I will be the happiest person alive," Alex whispered, holding my hand against his heart. I smiled as I felt his heartbeat and tapped my leg along with it. I turned to him and leaned in until we were just inches apart.

"I think I know why," I whispered back. I gently took his head into my hand and kissed him. I ended up wrapping my arms around him and let Alex's warm arms wrap around my waist. We finally let go and went to our beds, still looking at each other.

"That was a one time thing, Mr. Alex," I giggled, tears welling up in my eyes as I stared at him for what might be the last time.

"I know. Good night, Melissa. I'll see you later," Alex said. I nodded and we smiled at each other one last time before we rested our head on our pillows. I dreamt of seeing him again, and wondering if everything will be normal when I do.

Saturday, April 21, 2018.
7:10 in the morning.

I didn't wake up to an alarm, Alex's guitar playing, Ember's complaining, or Sabrine's critics on anyone's outfit. Instead, I woke up to the sounds of how silent the room and the hallways sounded. I slipped on my slippers and my robe and quietly unlocked and opened my door. There was no one in the hallways. I quickly walked through the empty hallways until I finally got to Jere's room. I quietly knocked on his door and was welcomed by Abree, Faye, and Jere. I ran into their arms and we all sat down on the floor together in silence.

"I can't believe they're all gone. It's just us four today," I mumbled, grabbing Jere and Faye's hands. We all walked out into the hallway and got our breakfast, trying our hardest to break the unbearable silence. On our way back, I decided it was time we did something with ourselves. I grabbed all of our new keys and threw them all to their new owners.

"We might as well move into our new rooms, and then we'll go together to move lockers," I suggested with nothing more than a sigh. The rest of them nodded and we went back to our rooms.

It felt really weird not having Sabrine pick out my clothes for me, so I tried to act like her. I sat on her bed and was about to talk like her, when I found a sticky note under her pillow. I laughed and pulled out a silk pink shirt, jeans, and the note also said that I should have a tight bun. I packed up all of my stuff and after a final look at my now empty room, I started to search for room R1. I ended up finding Jere there, splitting everything in half since we're sharing the bookshelf and the dresser. I smiled and we spent the next few minutes setting up everything to our clothes and our hobby objects. After much arguing and begging, I finally agreed to let Jere take the floor and so I can have the bed. We heard a knock and walked outside to see Abree and Faye waiting for us.

"We're not the first one's thinking of moving our things to our new lockers. Ms. Genie wants to see us," Abree groans. We all groan as we walked out of the building and into the school building. We entered Ms. Genie's room and sat down facing her grinning face.

"Good morning children! As you might've noticed, all of the other students and their stuff are gone except you four. They went back to their home because they're not as "special" as you guys. It will just be you four today but tomorrow, new kids will be coming. I want to make sure you welcome them kindly. Tomorrow you will get new schedules with the new kids for school on Monday. Other than that, same rules and expectations apply, agreed?" Ms. Genie asked. After a moment, we all nodded and before she could say anything else, we ran out of the rooms and to our lockers.

"I can't believe she thinks we bought that," I laughed as I started to take off the few pictures that I had in my original locker. I finished unloading my locker and as I walked back to my new locker, I could hear laughter near my new locker. I found Abree and Faye laughing at Jere, standing on top of a desk and pretending to be Ms. Genie. I dropped my stuff off at my locker and laughed as I joined them.

"They went back to their home because they're not as special as you guys," Jere bellowed in a high-pitched voice. I stood on the desk with him and pointed my finger at Abree and Faye.

"Other than that, same rules and expectations apply, agreed?" I shouted in the sweetest high-pitched voice I could have. Abree and Faye fell over in laughter, and Jere and I were trying to laugh without falling off of the wobbly desk.

Suddenly, we heard footsteps get closer and closer to our hallway and we hastened to our new lockers and started to actually put our stuff inside. It was Ms. Bea, walking by to get to the copy room. She smiled and once she passed, we finally breathed and started laughing all over again. We finally finished and sat down on the ground in a circle.

"I know we just got done with some hard work, but last one to their dorm room is a rotten student!" I yelled as I sprang up and raced to the entrance door. They all laughed/screamed and raced after me. We sprinted to the entrance door, out and back into the dorm rooms. I darted around the corner and the four of us ended up tripping over each other and falling in a heap. We cracked up and sat up looking at each other.

"Ok. After lunch, I want to take you somewhere. Make sure to bring your phone and some markers," I breathed. We gave each other mysterious grins and carefully nodded at each other. I gave them a peace sign in return and walked back to the library. Ms. Genie sat silently in the corner, sitting in the same place where I first got to know Simon. I slowly sat across from her and decided on what to say.

"Why are you doing this?" I decided to say, barely getting it out of my mouth. Ms. Genie didn't look at me for second, considering her options. I leaned back in my chair, thinking that I finally broke her, but she came back just as hard.

"How much do you know?" Ms. Genie hissed at me. I laughed and leaned in so that we were only glaring at each other as far as inches.

"What makes you think I know anything?" I snarled back. Ms. Genie scoffed at me and made sure her eyes burned into mine.

"I think you know something, unless you wouldn't confront me like this," Ms. Genie slowly answered. I thought to myself of how wrong and right she is. She's right, because I do know something, a lot of things actually. But she's wrong, because that's not why I confronted her. I confronted her because I wanted to know why my mom was doing this, especially if she "cared" about me.

"What's your first name, mom?" I questioned, rolling out the "mom" as I spoke. Ms. Genie leaned back in her chair again and smiled at me.

"Amy, my name is Amy," Ms. Genie answered. I smiled at her back and looked at her intensely.

"Well, let me tell you something, Amy. I believe your name means dearly loved in French, and from the 'information' that I know, you are the total opposite of that. I'll see you later," I spat at her dismissively as I walked out of the library and towards the food court.

"It's so silent. It feels really weird being the only four here," Faye whispered as we weaved through multiple tables, weirdly looking for a place to sit.

"You don't have to whisper, you know. We're the only people here. It feels a tiny bit lonely, but at least I don't have to get rainbow flavored Slushies during lunch every day," I muttered, sitting down and digging into my chicken alfredo.

"Well, look at the cutest group of four on the block. Good thing no one's watching, I think I'm gonna puke," a deep voice barked from behind us. I growled as this familiar voice creeped back into my head. I slowly turned and cursed as Shane stood before us.

"Shane, what the heck are doing here? Everyone got sent back except for the four of us," I spat, standing up. Shane smiles his fully evil smile and walked up towards me, grabbing my neck.

"Well, I guess our mom made a little exception, huh? Wanted her two adorable kids under the same roof," Shane snarled, shaking me with his powerful arms, "and by the way, you and I are in the same Science class together. See you guys at dinner," Shane whispered in my ear. He let go of me and I gasped as I fell backwards. Jere rushed beside me and my face started to red up as I relearned how to breathe.

"What is my brother doing here?" I exclaimed, finally sitting back in my seat and taking a long gulp of some soda.

"Wait, this Shane guy is your brother!? I thought Gale and Gavin were your only siblings!" Abree and Faye shouted. I slightly smiled and started unpeeling my banana.

"Shane is Ms. Genie's son, making him my half brother. Which really sucks," I sigh, biting into my banana. Abree nodded, but Faye didn't say anything. I smiled again and after finishing my lunch, quietly walked back to my room.

My Melissa,
Dinner is in five minutes. I hope you're ok and if you don't want to eat dinner with your brother, I'll bring your food to you. Just text me what you want to do.

Love ya♥♥
Jere

I sighed and with all my might, I stood up and strode into the cafeteria. I sat down with everyone and for a moment we had a delightful time eating dinner, but then Shane arrived and decided to sit right next to me. I moaned, but focused on my spaghetti and meatballs instead.

"So, how has everyone's day been?" Shane questioned, his delirious grin spreading across the table and around us.

"It was fantastic, until the devil showed up," Jere muttered. Shane's grin turned into a innocent frown and he wrapped his arm around me. I tried to shrug his arm off, but his arm stayed put, gripping my shoulder.

"Oh, is that because mean brother over here stole your girlfriend?" Shane asked. Jere slammed his fork down and shoved Shane off the picnic table from across all the food. I quickly kicked him in the ribs and the four of us ran with our food back to our dorms.

"I'm sorry you guys had to sit with my brother. He's a jerk," I mumbled after we had made sure the door was locked and we were all settled with a movie and our food.

"No, I'm sorry. If I hadn't pushed him and just held in my anger, things would've been fine and we wouldn't have had to leave," Jere sighed, kissing my forehead. I waved him off and held his hand.

"It's ok. He deserved it, one. Two, this is so much better," I smiled. After while, we had finished dinner and it was time to head to bed. We wanted Abree and Faye to sleep over, but our friends will appear in the middle of the night, so we shouldn't. I lay on the foot side of my bed and grinned at my Jere lying below me. I take his hands in mine and hold them gingerly.

"Melissa, are you scared?" Jere whispered. I smiled and brought his hands to my chest, to my heartbeat.

"I'm terrified, Jere. But as long as I'm with you, I'm not scared at all," Jere smiled and I leaned down and lightly kissed him on the lips. As I fell asleep, I knew that as long as I'm not scared, I can accomplish anything.

Sunday, April 22, 2018.
6:35 in the morning.

The lovely chirping of the birds outside my window and the soft first rays of sunshine on my face woke me up, warming me up to a beautiful day. I saw Jere was still sleeping peacefully below me, and across the room slept Lacey, Kennedy, and Rosemary. I beamed with happiness once I saw them. I crept out of bed and snuck out of the room. By the time I got to the breakfast table, my feet were chilled to the bone. I picked out food and I placed everyone's food next to the tv. Today I decided to wear a flowery orange tank top, dark jeans, and a mix of orange, blue, and pink heels. I sat on my bed and watched as the the sunrise rose high above and into the sky.

"Melissa? Is that you?" Kennedy muttered behind me. I turned and I was suddenly racing towards Kennedy and falling on top of her.

"Kennedy! It's you! I've missed you so much, you have no idea!" I cried, hugging her and hugging her close. Kennedy smiled and soon we were both laughing. So enough, Rosemary, Lacey, and Jere woke up and we all got ready and ate breakfast together. Minutes later, we ran over to rooms R2 and R3 and soon we were all reunited again, hugging close in a big group hug.

"Can I tell you that it feels so good to be with you guys again. I haven't felt this happy in a while," Jere said proudly, grinning.

"Now, I have an idea that we can do as a group to start this reunion off right! I have another brother named Shane, Ms. Genie's son. He's also here, in room R4. I say we put whip cream and blueberries all over him and then sprint to a place he doesn't know about. Don't worry, I stole his keys last night. You guys with me?" I inquired, rubbing my hands together in a mysterious way. Everyone else grinned and we started our mission. Amber, Trent, Faye, and Lucy set out to find blueberries and whip cream. Lacey, Belle and I went to the secret place and got ready for everyone else to come running through. Samira, Gavin and Kennedy were going to break in, do the prank and sneak out. Jere, Rosemary, and Abree are going to write the note that we will leave for Shane.

"Ok. You can start the prank now, we're ready," I whispered through my walkie talkie as Lacey and Belle closely followed me out of the dorm building and towards the secret place.

"Here it is guys. Our secret place," I grinned, unlocking the door and leading them through the room. Lacey and Belle gasped at the wonderful view of the glowing markers and the gallery of people on the floor. I smiled at them and walked back to the door to unlock it for everyone else. But the door was stuck, and it wouldn't move.

"Belle, Lacey, come help me with the door. It's jammed," I groaned, trying to yank the door open. Lacey and Belle rushed over and pulled on the door with me. It still wouldn't move.

"It's either tightly jammed or locked. Where are they going to go?" Belle asked, sitting up and resting her body against the wall. I shrugged in hopelessness and slid down the wall. I stared at the glowing wall in front of us and smiled at the multicolor light. But out of nowhere, a red marker was writing huge words across the wall; no one was holding the marker.

"Guys, check this out," I murmured, slowly standing up. Lacey and Belle followed me and we gazed up at what the red marker was writing.

"Choose wisely who you choose to hang out with," Lacey, Belle, and I said, reading the written words off the wall, "secrets can be shared, and some people shouldn't be hearing them. Good luck jerks! -C," We finished, staring at each other in bewilderment.

"What does that mean?" Lacey exclaimed. Belle shrugged and picked up an abandoned axe in the corner.

"I have no idea, but I'm not sticking around to find out," Belle grumbled, lifting the axe and breaking the door. Lacey and I grabbed two more axes and started to hit the door as well until a hole big enough to get through was revealed. Just then, Jere, Amber, Samira, Kennedy, Rosemary, Trent, Gavin, Abree, Faye, and Lucy came sprinting through the hole and falling to the ground. Lacey, Belle, and I started to laugh and started to help them up.

"OMG! You should've been there, Melissa. That was epic! I even got a picture," Gavin grinned, walking over to me and showing me a picture of

Shane on his phone. I beamed with pleasure and walked over to the hole/door.

"That's awesome! But let's go. It's about time for lunch and we have a lot to talk about. None of that needs to happen here," I breathed, ushering everyone back outside and towards the cafeteria.

"Ok guys. Belle, Lacey and I found a very interesting and creepy note in the secret place. I got a bad feeling it has something to do with us," I explained, sitting down with everyone as I started to dig into my burger.

"We were locked inside for a moment, and we saw this red marker writing on the wall. But no one was holding the marker! It wrote, "Choose wisely who you choose to hang out with. Secrets can be shared, and some people shouldn't be hearing them. Good luck jerks! - C.," Belle added.

"Well, minus that fact that this note is basically telling us to choose our friends and something about secrets, I think we should be more concerned of who 'C' is," Jere murmured, squeezing tightly on his soda can.

"Attention students! I, Mrs. Genie, is here to give you your schedule and give an announcement," Mrs. Genie announced, standing in front of the food line, handing out the schedules that were in her hand.

"Ok, now for the announcement. The very few of you are still here because you are special. You are going to be tested, individually and in groups, to see what is special about you.

Melissa, you will be tested tomorrow during your Science class. Come to my office. Thank you and have a nice rest of your day," Mrs. Genie finished, grinning the most despicable smile as she strolled out of the cafeteria. I shrugged, shoved the last of my brownie into my mouth, and ran out of the cafeteria and back to the dorm rooms.

"Hey, what's wrong?" Jere asked, walking over to our bed and sitting down next to me. I wiped my tears away and leaned against his shoulder.

"I don't know, Jere," I sighed, looking up into his eyes, "I just thought that I, that we can get through this. But now I'm so scared for tomorrow. I just what you, Marvin, Gale, and my parents," I sobbed. I fell back on the bed and let my tears melt into the soft pillow. Jere didn't say anything, he just wrapped his arms around me and rocked me until there were no more tears left. Jere lifted me back up and took my hand in his.

"Come on, I have a surprise for you," Jere whispered. I smiled and walked with him outside. A few minutes later, we were walking the trail towards the lake. I knew that we weren't allowed to go to the lake, but didn't want anything to get in the way of my speck of hopefulness and happiness. Jere walked me over to the middle of the bridge, smiled, and went to the other end of the lake.

While I waited, I stared up at the sky. The sun was setting and the crisp soft wind ran through my hair and across my face. I breathed out a smile and felt the calmness around me as I closed my eyes. Abruptly, I felt a gentle breeze across the peaceful lake. I opened my eyes and gasped at what I saw.

Lucy, Lacey, Faye, Abree, Gavin, Trent, Kennedy, Belle, Samira, Rosemary, and Amber stood around the small lake, holding lantern balloons. Jere was on the end of the bridge ahead of me, holding 2 lantern balloons in his hands. Jere walked towards me with his charming tie, meeting me at the center of the bridge with a smile. He took my hand and got down on one knee as I started to tear up.

"Melissa, I love you, and I think I always will. I know this sound crazy coming from a 7th grader, but I think I want to marry you, someday. This is a promise ring. I know that only high schoolers and adults do this kind of stuff, but if you wear it, I promise to love you, support you, and care for you in every situation possible. I promise to always be there for you and to cherish you. If at anytime that I don't do that, you can take it off. Maybe when we're a lot older and you're still wearing it, we can be together. Will you take this promise ring again, Melissa?" Jere asked, taking my promise ring out of his pocket and holding it out in front of me. I was so overwhelmed with happiness and tears that I just nodded and held out my hand. Jere slipped the ring back on my finger, where it belonged, and lifted me into the air. Everybody cheered and on the count of three, they threw their balloons into the air.

"You got this back? I thought you gave this to Rosemary. Guess you broke up with her," I whisper with a small smile. Jere just shrugged, and I grinned back.

"Thank you, for being to best boyfriend and friend I can ever have," I smiled, holding him close. Jere beamed back, and we lifted our balloons into the air, watching them float into the sky with everyone else's. Before another second can pass by, I turned Jere's face back to me and leaned in for a kiss. I wrapped my arms around him and let his arms slowly wrap around my waist.

Out of nowhere, the bridge started to loudly creak beneath us. I slowly pulled away, and with Jere's arms still wrapped tightly around me, we slowly stared down at the bridge. Everybody cautiously advanced unto the bridge with us, making the bridge creak even louder.

"Guys, get off!!" I suddenly yelled. Throughout the entire bridge, deafening snaps hurt my ears, and all of a sudden the bridge broke in half. We all screamed as we plummeted into the water. Before we could react to anything, multiple colors started to glow in the water and around us. I gaped at the colors, shining brightly on my face. Before we could fully process what was going on *then*, the gleaming colors disappeared. All we could do was awkwardly giggle at each other and quickly run out of the lake and back to the dorm building before anyone could see us. After drying up and snuggling up in bed, I felt kinda weird to my stomach.

"Jere, do you feel a little strange?" I called out to him, twisting my hands together until they turned very pale. Jere sat up to face me and rested his head at the end of my bed.

"Yes. I think everyone does. It's probably just the lake water. Good night Melissa," Jere whispered back, smiling before lying back down. I smiled and laid down as well, trying my hardest to forget the strange feeling.

Monday, April 23, 2018.
6:04 in the morning.

I slowly woke up to the soft alarm and the beautiful chirps outside, but stopped when I looked around at myself and everyone else in the room. My body was glowing a very faint cyan color. I look down at Jere and his body is glowing a light cornflower blue color. Kennedy was glowing a faint green, Rosemary was glowing a light red, and Lacey was glowing a faint pink. I slowly get up and pull on a white and cyan tank top, black and white striped jeans, and converses like everything was normal. I got all ready for school and gently woke everyone else. Everyone noticed the glow first thing when they opened their eyes but acted more startled than I was.

"What the heck is going on?" Rosemary started, sitting up and pacing in panic. I run over to Jere and back to Kennedy, starting to pace back and forth across the room.

"I don't know. I knew the lake water felt wrong, I knew it," I mumbled, running my hands through my hair. Jere nodded and sat me down in a chair so that my legs would stop shaking.

"Um, guys. We got another note from "C". It knows what happened to us," Lacey whispered, standing up and walking towards a dark red note dripping on our wall.

"Like the new glow? It's your new powers. Try some out! Some of you can fly. Some of you can run very fast, some of you can control what they've always wanted to control, and some of you can be the evil they were always meant to be. Just one tip: Don't get caught. - C," we all murmured. I sighed, told everyone to meet me at lunch and spread the word, and headed out for class.

Now with only fourteen of us enrolled in the school and we don't have all the same classes together, it felt like a awkward, really small private school. Having L.A class with just Samira and Lucy was really weird yet interesting. But what was more creepy was the fact that Samira was glowing a dark green and Lucy was shining a faint yellow, not to mention my very noticeable cyan color. Although S.S. and Spanish class were actually kinda fun, seeing Kennedy, Gavin, Faye, and Lucy shine colors of green, orange, purple, and yellow were not the fun parts. As lunch approached, all of us quickly got our lunches and nervously sat down.

"Ok. Can someone tell me what the heck is with the new gleam, and what's with the note C gave us?" Trent asked curiously, his light blue hand shaking as he poured his sauce over his salad.

"About the glow, I'm not exactly sure. It might have something to do with the lake, when it glowed around us? For the note, I assume we each have some sort of power? I'm going to try whatever mine is during Free Period at the field beyond the lake. But until then, let's just be careful," I suggested, picking at my food as well. Soon enough, the bell for class rang and Lacey, Rosemary, Amber, and I decided to go to the field to figure out what was going on. Once at the field, I pulled out a written copy of the note C gave us.

"Like the new glow? It's your new powers. Try some out! Some can fly. Some can run very fast, some can control what they've always wanted to control, some can be the evil they were always meant to be. Just one tip: Don't get caught. -C," I read carefully.

"Well, it's simple, I guess, for the first part. Some of us can at least fly, and the others can at least run very fast, like the Flash. But I don't know about the third one. Maybe we can try flying and running and see what we have?" Rosemary started, walking to the middle of the field. She got in running position and she suddenly started running towards the mountains in the distance. She wasn't going the speed of light, so I assumed she couldn't run fast. I smiled and anxiously walked towards the middle as well. *Ok Melissa. Think. Think of flying, the way the wind races through you and how your heart drops with excitement.* I thought. I breathed, closed my eyes and thought of this, smiling at these images.

"Melissa, Melissa! You're flying!" Lacey screamed. I opened my eyes and gasped, my body being just a little over 6 feet off the ground. I smiled, bent my knees and leaped higher into the sky, zipping through the sky. Amber and Rosemary smiled and flew up with me. Lacey instead started running like the speed of light, maybe even faster.

I smiled and as I swept through the clouds, I had one of those moments where everything is simple and free.

"Guys, the bell rang! Let's go or we'll be late!" Amber suddenly yelled. We all glanced at each other and sped back towards the school. I rushed by my locker and ran into Science class.

After class, Shane tripped me and my stuff went tumbling. I scowled at him but just picked up my stuff and continued my journey to Math class. But Shane didn't stop. He ran in front of me and punched my stuff back out of my hands. Instead of grabbing my stuff again, I punched him in the gut, knocking him backwards.

"You're such a creep. What do you want now?" I snapped, quickly grabbing my stuff. Shane softly groaned but smiled at me as he walked forwards again.

"You're the creep, Melissa. You are the one who started it all. Not only did you create this stupid curse over your school, but you are the one that made mom leave you and your dad. If you had just been perfect, mom would've stayed, you would act like a normal child, and no one would have to deal with your idiotic crap every 5 minutes! But no, you just had to come out like this. Why don't you do us a favor and just disappear!" Shane snarled. That's when my final nerve snapped. My hands quickly turned into fists, making them glow even brighter. Instead of my fighting thoughts storming in, a new source of empowerment came in. Just then, I remembered a part of the "C" note. *Some can control what they've always wanted to control.*

I stare at Shane and thought about an animal that he probably hates: spiders. I closed my eyes and thought about all of the spiders and cobwebs that lurk and hide in the nooks and crannies at this school. Then I imagined all of them crawling and sticking against him, pushing him against the lockers. I hear a muffled scream and open my eyes in shock and true pleasure.

Shane was screaming as around 20 huge spiders crawled up and around him, cobwebs sticking to his mouth. I laughed and walked up to him, cautious of the mess.

"Um, I'm sorry? Last time I checked, I prefer being locked in a room for an hour listening to my own crap than deal with **your** idiotic crap! Why don't you do everyone a favor and head to your next class. Oh wait, you can't. See ya bro!" I smirked, walking away right when the bell rang for class to start.

"Jere! Amber, Lacey, Rosemary and I found out something amazing!" I said happily, rushing into my room. Jere jumped up in surprise as I burst in with energy.

"Ok! Ok! You do realize that you missed your test with Ms. Genie, right?" Jere asked, walking up to me.

"Oh, right! I don't give crap about that. Get everyone together and meet us at the field beyond the lake!" I finished, giving him a kiss and racing into the hallway, back towards the field.

Few minutes later, all of us were gathered in a circle in the middle of the field. After Gavin reread the note, I beamed and walked to the middle of the circle. I closed my eyes once again and imagined my hair blowing behind me as I flew through the clouds. I opened my eyes and smiled as I zipped around and under the clouds. My friends looked up at me in shock and pleasure, cheering me on. Rosemary and Amber joined me, while Lacey showed off her amazing running skills.

Two hours later, the 13 of us were walking back to the dorms in absolute delight. Gavin and I found out that we can fly and can control objects and the mind. Jere found out that he can run very fast and is very strong, carrying the rest of us without a sweat. Amber and Trent found out that they can fly and are very smart, able to find the answers to all of our difficult math problems. Samira and Abree found out that they can run very fast and are very, very flexible. Belle and Faye found out that they can fly and they have lasers in their eyes and hands. Kennedy and Lacey found out that they can run very fast and can turn invisible. Finally, Rosemary and Lucy found out that they can fly and have the ability to transform into other people, creating clones of all of us. We rushed back in our rooms and as everyone was getting ready to head to dinner, I got a text. Surprisingly, it was a text from Shane.

Melissa,
I want to talk to you. At the secret place.
Yes, I know where that is. Don't worry, I'm
not doing this to pay you back. I deserved
those spiders and cobwebs. If you trust me,
meet me there right before dinner, bringing
nobody. Hope I see you there.

Shane

I leaned against the bedpost and sighed. *Do I trust him?* I thought. I don't trust him, I definitely don't need to trust him, but I really want to trust him. I have Jere and my lifelong friends, but without Marvin, Gale, dad, or Teresa to be with, Shane is all that I have left. I don't trust him, so I'm going to go see if I can.

"Hey, are you coming to dinner?" Samira asked, sitting next to me. I nodded and pointed to Jere.

"I just need to get something done. I'll meet you guys there. Can you save a bite for me if I'm that late? Jere will know what to get," I sighed. Samira smiled, hugged me close, and headed out with everyone else. Once everyone was outside, I gradually walked out of the building and glided to the secret place. I ducked through the ripped up hole and saw Shane sitting up against the wall where we got the first note from C.

"So, you trust me?" Shane asked. I scoffed at him and leaned against the wall across from him.

"Every vein in my body doesn't trust you. I *want* to trust you, so I came to see if I can. Is that ok?" I inquired. Shane nodded, his face expression dazed but unworried.

"Why do you want to trust me? I thought that we were enemies," Shane remembered, rubbing his hands together. I crossed my arms and looked up at his dark brown eyes.

"Because I need a brother right now. Ms. Genie is definitely not in my family category, but you can be, and should be. I wanted to see if I can let you in with everyone else. I can't let somebody into my family category if I can't trust them, right?" I answered.

"I want to let you in as well. I know that this probably won't shock you, but I don't consider Ms. Genie in my family category either. She's a horrible mother. I don't have anyone else, except you," Shane muttered. I stood up and looked at him more intensely.

"What about your dad?" I asked. Shane looked up at me, tears in his eyes.

"He left me a week after I was born, just like our mom left you a week after you were born. I don't remember what he looks like, probably because at the time my eyes weren't fully opened. Mom told me that it was my fault, but I know she said that because she felt hurt. I felt so bad for her because she told me that you and your dad left her.

166

All my life I thought she was this innocent woman, and all that she did was for a reason. But now, I know I thought wrong. The only reason I have for being on mom's side is because she's the only family I have left, besides you. Letting go of her, I have no family left," Shane whispered, sinking down to the floor. I sat down next to him and held his hand in mine.

"I'm your family now. Just the two of us, family. Now I do trust you, with every vein in my body," I smiled, and together, hand in hand, we walked back to the dorm building and into the cafeteria.

"Melissa, why are you holding Shane's hand? Is he controlling you?" Jere quietly yelled, running up to me once we got inside.

"I thought you were a witness when I figured out that I can control minds? He's not controlling me, and everything's fine. Shane and I are family now. We always were, but we let what's going on right now get in the way. He's on our side. He has no reason not to be," I responded. Shane smiled and we all sat down for dinner together.

"Ok, I have a few inner points on what's going on around here, and I'd be happy to share them with you. But I'm not opening my mouth until I know I'm respected and that all of you trust me," Shane said, slowly opening and drinking from his soda. The others nodded and we just continued eating in silence. We all finished quickly and left the cafeteria and towards the dorms without saying a word, afraid we were all going to turn around and stab each other. When I got back, I got a text from Ms. Genie.

I groaned as I fell unto the bed. Jere came over and wrapped me up in his arms. I breathed slowly and leaned against him, letting my pressure rest.

"I have to take the test tomorrow, and I have to do it for at most 3 days without any classes or interaction with peers. I have to pack up my stuff and live with Ms. Genie during the testing. I have to leave the dorms in 20 minutes. I'm so scared, Jere," I breathed. Jere held me closer and rocked me back and forth, but the tears didn't stop from coming.

"Everything is going to be alright, Melissa. Me, Shane, and everyone will be right here if you need anything. We will always be with you. We have powers, don't we?" Jere smiled tiredly at me. I nodded and stood up, heading towards the door.

"Ok. I think I'm going to visit Shane before I leave. I'll be back in a minute," My voice sounding distant as I closed the door and hurried towards Shane. I quietly knocked on his door and as soon as Shane opened the door, I welled up with tears again. I told him everything and Shane casually pulled me into a hug, and I didn't resist. I my legs suddenly went limp and I was grasping at Shane, tears damping our shirts and blurring my eyes. Shane kept me until I finally regained myself, and everyone came back to my room to help me pack. After everything was set and kisses and hugs were shared, I stood at the door with my suitcase and a slight smile in hand.

"Bye guys. I'll miss you all. Do me a favor, be brave and strong. When I can't do it for myself, I know you'll do it for me. See you in a few days," I sighed, waving at them and wandered out of the dorm building and towards Ms. Genie's office. I knocked on Mrs. Genie's office and balloons and streamers greeted me as I walked in.

"Welcome! I can't wait for this. We are going to have so much fun," Ms. Genie exclaimed as she grabbed my stuff and placed them on the bed in the next room, which must be where she lives.

"What the heck? I'm just staying here for the tests. I wake up, take tests all day, and go back to bed. There is no 'we' in that. Night," I scoffed, grabbing a blanket and pillow and laid down on the floor without changing, trying to imagine that I'm with Jere and not with my despicable mother.

Tuesday, April 24, 2018.
5:30 in the morning.

All of a sudden, an alarm shook up my insides and ears as I quickly jumped to my feet. I looked around, finding Ms. Genie asleep, balloons and streamers still on the ground, and that it was 5:30 in the morning. I quietly groaned and started to pick through my clothes. I decided on a purple shirt with black drawings on it, black jeans, and dark gray boots. I promptly went to get myself breakfast and read for another 20 minutes until Ms. Genie finally decided to get up.

"When's the first test?" I asked. Ms. Genie lifted her head from her pillow and smiled as she gradually stood up and walked to her desk.

"Now. Guards, take her to the laboratory," Ms. Genie smirked. I looked at her in confusion when rough hands grabbed my arms and tied them behind my back. There was a minute of shock, but I just laughed and stared at her with uncertainty.

"Thank you. Really, why do you need to tie my hands? Just because I don't want to take the tests doesn't mean I'm gonna go anywhere," I complained.

"Well, I guess we'll just have to see, won't we? I heard that my tests can be, terrifying. Have fun," Ms. Genie smirked, waving me off as they dragged me out of the room and towards the lab.

What looked like men untied my hands and practically threw me into a room with bright lights, lots of computers, and a single chair. The men then left the room, locking the door behind them. At the other side of the room, there was another room that was separated by glass, like an observatory room. I figured I can just stand there until they let me out and I won't have to take the test, but then, a voice out of nowhere told me sit down. I gradually sat down and a huge helmet-like machine went over my head.

"We are now going to start the test. You will be put under certain situations. Depending on what your reactions are to those situations, we will find out exactly who you are. The only tools you will have are a knife and a feather. Good luck," a light female voice announced. I sighed and calmly settled in as a light green smoke surround me. Soon enough, I fell asleep.

I wake up in a dark room, covered in dust. I look around to see that there are no windows or furniture, I have a feather and a thick, sharp knife in my hands, and that there was a door at the far end of the room. I quickly walked over to the door and turned the doorknob, but it was locked. I shrugged, but tensed right back up when I heard a low growl behind me. I slowly turned around and shivered at what was standing at the other end of the room.

A huge, pitch black dog was standing there, teeth bared. I was about to run, or kill the dog, when a thought came to me. *This isn't real. It's just Ms. Genie's stupid test.* I calmly straightened my back and started to walk towards the dog. The dog barked and started to charge at me. I jumped a little, but tried my hardest to stay still. The dog opened his mouth wide and I closed my eyes as he bit at my stomach. But he didn't.

The dog ran through me, like I was a ghost! The dog jumped through me, biting and clawing at the air. Once the dog was on the other side of me, it disappeared. I slightly smiled for a moment, spinning around to unlock the door with the end of the feather. I opened the door and walked into another large, bare room. The room was all white, with puddles of water scattered around the place. At the end of the room was the legendary Simon.

"Come and get me, Melissa! I know you want to. Let's see if Ms. Slushie Slut here can actually get near me with all of her beverages.

Good luck!" Simon snarled. I laughed but then stopped when I realized that my hands and feet were tied together, the feather and knife laying on the ground. I groaned, but casually shuffled towards him.

All of a sudden, the walls spewed out all kinds of Slushie into my face and all over my body. I screamed as it chilled my body and attacked my insides, Simon ushered me forward with a wicked smile. I kept on moving towards him as more and more Slushies came in. At one point, my body gave up and I crumpled up against the floor.

"Come on, wimp! Slushies can't get you down, your Ms. Slushie Slut!" Simon bellowed. I grimaced and continued to crawl until I stopped breathlessly at a puddle. I looked over the puddle and saw my reflection, red and green Slushie dripping down my face. I breathed through my nose and thought about the room I was in earlier. *This is not real.* I breathed in again and put my face into the water. My body came with me until I was fully underwater. I smiled and swam up to the top with pride.

I sat up in shock and looked around me. I was back in the room with the chair, but everything was destroyed. The chair was battered and everything in the room shook and sparked with electricity. I shivered with astonishment and excitement in my seat as I saw Ms. Genie stare at me in fright, the glass shattered and everything on the other side, including her, burned to a black crisp.

"Um – th...thank you, Melissa. You will won't need to take any more tests like we originally said. You are free go collect your things and head back to your dorm before dinner. You will return to school tomorrow," Ms. Genie murmured through the mic below her. I sat there in fright for a moment longer, then rushed out of the room, not looking back. I quickly grabbed my things from Ms. Genie's office and raced back to the dorm building. I spotted Jere and Shane near the library and I couldn't contain my excitement.

"Shane! Jere!" I screamed. I dropped my stuff and started to run over to them when all of a sudden, I felt really queasy to my stomach. After a few steps I fell on my knees and then my stomach, hugging my arms and cursing through my tightened teeth. Shane and Jere rushed towards me, holding me up with their shaking arms.

"Melissa? Melissa, are you ok? What happened?" Shane begged, Jere squeezing my hand. I put my hand on Jere's face and smiled with the last of my energy.

"I.. need.. to.. rest," I muttered, trying to keep consistent breaths. Jere and Shane immediately nodded and started to lift me up. They swiftly carried me through the halls and when Gavin and Trent saw us, they quickly got my bags and followed us. I lay on my bed and I fell asleep right away, the worry leaving me just as fast.

Wednesday, April 25, 2018.
6:07 in the morning.

My body slowly woke up to the beautiful morning that creeped through the windows, but I was definitely not ready to wake up. I dragged myself out of bed, lazily pulling on a peach shirt, ripped jeans, brown heels and pushed myself through the hallways and down to school. The only thing that kept me awake during each class was controlling people to do stupid things or having certain objects like pencils and erasers fly across the room. For example, having me <u>and</u> Gavin in the same Spanish Class with both of us able to control minds and objects was pretty chaotic and awesome.

"Ok, I have understood that all of you fully trust me, so let's cut down to the chase," Shane started, sitting down with the rest of us during lunch, "Ms. Genie knows that there is a map that leads to one of the main parts of her plan, other than you guys. She just can't find the map," Shane ended in confusion. I shrugged and continued to eat my pizza. My napkin suddenly flew off the table and as I swept down to grab it, I saw this shining red stripe on the ground. There was also a letter that was hidden on the inside of the napkin. I hastened to pick it up and slowly read it aloud to the rest of the group.

"You're running out of time. I know that green usually means go, but this time **<u>red</u>** means go. Follow the red stripes or else the only stripes you'll see will be on your official "Death Call" outfit. -C" I breathed with butterflies zooming around in my stomach.

"Well, I know that I'm not staying here all my life with the "Death Call" printed all over me, so let's go!" Faye hissed, throwing her food away and starting to head out of the food court.

"What about class? What do you think will happen if we <u>ditch</u> the rest of the school day when someone called the "Death Call" is in charge?" Lucy argued back, standing up and blocking the food court exit.

"I don't think we have much of a choice at this point. It's now or never. Plus, I think that's the map that Ms. Genie is looking for," Faye said urgently. The rest of us nodded and with that, we raced out of the food court, following the glistening red stripes. The ribbons of radiant red lead us all the way out of the school building and into the secret place. We walked inside and immediately saw a note written in dark red, covering the wall.

"Think about home. What makes your home, home. Look for those things, and soon enough, you'll actually find your home. -C" We all whispered. I breathed and started to think about moments and objects that made me think of home.

I remember Teresa waking me and the boys up at 1 in the morning on dad's birthday and we spent all morning jamming to cool music and baking every dessert we knew how to make. We then hid around the kitchen and when he came down, we scared the crap out of him. Dad spent the rest of his day eating all of the pastries while the rest of took multiple naps throughout the day. I smiled as that memory and others came into my mind, and we started to look for these memories. We finally stopped looking when we found a hidden corner at the back of the room. It was tunnel, and inside of it was a swirling mixture of numerous colors, with various pictures surrounding it.

"These are pictures of our families," Belle breathed, drawing her finger around her face in a picture, "and pictures of our favorite family memories." I nodded and slowly walked up to one of my memory pictures. It was a picture of dad, Teresa, Marvin, Gale, and myself up in the mountains at our cabin. That was my favorite memory of our family. We went swimming, hiking, and had so much fun together. That was around 5 months before she left.

"Guys, look. Another note," Trent exclaimed a little nervously as he ripped off a note that was sticking at the bottom of the hole. Trent read it and then looked up at us, scared and frantic.

"I think we might want to go back to our dorms and sit down while we read this," Trent muttered, staring back down at the paper and nothing else. After a minute, we nodded and raced back to the dorms. Once we were safe in my room, I slowly took the note from Trent and read it aloud.

"If you are reading this, you have found the portal. The hole that you saw can take you back home. But you can't leave yet. Ms. Genie plans on destroying you and your school. For what reason, I'm not sure. You'll have to figure that out. You have to also get key that activates the weapon.

If you leave the "Death Call" without the key, you will be destroyed. Once you get the key, go straight home and destroy the key where this all started before Ms. Genie finds you. You have 3 days. Good luck. -C" I said. I threw the note to the ground and buried my face into my hands.

"So, let me get this right. We just found a portal that can take us home and away from all of this mess and we can't leave?" Amber and Rosemary shouted.

"We'll still be in the mess if we leave now. We'll be having to deal with this stuff when we get back, just like it was before. We have to get the key from her, go back home, and destroy the key where it all started, right?" Abree asked. I lifted my head and quickly sneaked a look at Amber and Jere.

"Where it all started, where it all started! Amber, Jere, where did we go when we first started to play the game in 3rd grade?" I murmured.

"We started it at the Eiffel Tower jungle gym thing. That's where you and Amber were taken and I saved you. Does the note mean that we have to destroy the key there?" Jere answered. I nodded and sat down on the floor with everyone else.

"Ok, guys. This is it. If we do it right, we can finish this and things can go back to normal. Let's make a plan and get to work. I don't know about you guys, but tonight is my last night here," I decided with a little smirk. Everyone else agreed and we started to get to work.

After another hour, we finally had a plan. Tonight, Gavin and Trent are going to create a distraction while I go into Ms. Genie's office and get 6 school keys. Then, tomorrow morning, we will pack our bags to get ready to leave. During my Free Period, Samira, Amber, Lucy, Gavin, and Lacey will get everyone's bags and go to the secret place to guard the portal and be ready to push our bags through. Faye, Belle, Trent, Faye, and Shane will go to the five entrances/exits of the school and will get ready to lock the doors to keep Ms. Genie inside while we run. Last but not least, Rosemary, Abree, Kennedy, and I will get the key. I got my purse and headed out with Gavin and Trent towards Ms. Genie's office. The boys positioned themselves in one locker hallway while I hid in the girl's bathroom.

"What the heck are you doing, stealing my girl away from me! You know that Kennedy is mine!" Gavin suddenly yelled, pushing Trent against the lockers.

"You're not the only one innocent, Gavin! What's with the picnic and the cute selfies with my girl, Lacey!" Trent shouted back, almost punching him in the face as he shoved him against a billboard. I started to get worried, until I heard heels pacing down the hallway.

"Boys! Boys! Break it up! What do you say for yourselves? Come on, let's go talk in the library," Ms. Genie said urgently, softly pushing them down the hallway. I grinned and ran in the other direction towards her office.

Luckily, Ms. Genie labels everything, so I could easily find 5 keys to lock all of the doors. But finding the weapon key was a bit harder. The only reason it didn't take me forever to find it was because a light blue color was shining through a box under her desk. I quickly lifted the lid and found it. It looked more like a spiky crystal than a key, but I knew that was it. I quickly put the box back where I found it and ran back to the dorm building. I gave the keys to the people who needed them and walked over to Rosemary, Abree, and Kennedy.

"The key is in this box underneath her desk. When we get the key, we just need to be careful because Ms. Genie might be in there while we're doing it. Kennedy's invisible, so she'll get the key, and the rest of will be ready to close the door on Ms. Genie and fly/run as fast as we can. Alright?" I questioned. Everyone nodded and we all stood up to go and get Gavin and Trent.

"What was so big of a distraction that you almost got a detention?" Lacey smirked as we met up with them in front of the doors to the cafeteria. Gavin and Trent had detention warning stickers on them, giving them a strike 1.

"We were pushing each other in the hallway, fighting about how we stole each other's girlfriends," Gavin said, trying his hardest to keep in his giggles.

"Who were your girlfriends?" Shane asked. Trent stopped in front of the cafeteria doors and pointed at Lacey and Kennedy.

"Kennedy was Gavin's girlfriend and Lacey was mine," Trent answered, bracing himself against the door. Kennedy's and Lacey's faces immediately switched to red and they chased the boys into the cafeteria. The rest of us laughed and after a moment we followed them inside, suddenly stopping in astonishment.

Lacey, Kennedy, Trent, and Gavin were on opposite sides of the room, tables turned on their sides as shields, and throwing food at each other. I shrieked as pieces of broccoli flew past me and before I knew what I was doing, I ran over to Lacey and Kennedy's base. People started to join sides until it was a full out food fight. We were throwing food until our clothes and hair were drenched in food and we smelled revolting. After we washed up and finally had an actual dinner, Shane pulled me aside as we walked back towards the dorm building and lead me to the lake instead.

"Melissa, what's going to happen after we leave? What will happen to our mom?" Shane asked. I shrugged and sat down next to the lake.

"I don't know. I feel like she still has some good in her, it just has been buried for too long. I don't feel comfortable leaving her, but I don't think of her as my mom," I explained. Shane just nodded. I looked at him with my "we-don't-have-another-choice" face, but all Shane did was frown as he sat next to me.

"Melissa, I hope you understand. If we leave our mom, I will have nothing left. No family," Shane begged, trying to keep it together. I grabbed his hands and pulled him closer to me, wiping a tear off his face.

"Breathe, and listen to me. **You don't need her**. You won't be alone. I'm your family! If you're my family, then you're my family's family as well. We'll see what we can do when we get back. All I know is that you don't need to be with her. Come on, we need some good rest. We have a big day tomorrow," I slightly pleaded, tugging his arm. Shane nodded and followed me away from the lake, away from our confusion. I kiss Jere on his forehead before I climb into my bed. I hear Jere's heartbeat and grin, slowing my heartbeat down to match his.

"Are you scared to go back home? With your family and all?" Jere whispered into the dark. I sighed glanced through the open window, looking at the stars and feeling the soft breeze surround me.

"Not really. I'm actually really excited! I have missed Teresa so much and just us as a family, being together. I don't want yet another thing getting in the way of my family, not now, when we're just rebuilding things," I answered. All I get in response is a chuckle and with that, I close my eyes and wish for the best.

Thursday, April 26, 2018.
6:08 in the morning.

Everyone wakes up around the same time to the annoying alarm, but no one says a word. We all slowly wake up and start to pack up all of our stuff together. I can feel the nervous energy surrounding us as I pull on a blue shirt, black and white sprinkled jeans, converses and quickly walk to class. The clock ticked every second, every minute, making every class longer than the first, but every class whizzed by for me. All I could think about is the key and what would happen, especially if I didn't get the key. Knowing Ms. Genie and what she can do, I kept on getting more and more nervous as the day went on.

Unfortunately, lunch arrived shortly and I was shaking as I spooned myself some plain yogurt with granola.

"Melissa, are you ok? You seem a little shaken up," Jere asked, wrapped his arm around my shoulder. My shivers multiplied times 10 as I shook my hand and leaned against his shoulder.

"I'm just really nervous about we're about to do. If we get caught, I can feel that one of us is going to get hurt in some way or another. I'm just scared," I mumbled. Jere hugged me close and held my arms tightly so that my shaking eased down.

"It's ok to be scared, Melissa! I bet you that everyone here is scared about doing this. But we will all be fine <u>because</u> we are doing this together, as a team. We got this," Jere said assuredly. I nodded and quickly kissed him on the cheek. Before Jere or anyone else can do anything else, I waved everyone to their positions as the class bell rang. After a few moments of silence, I stood up with Rosemary, Abree, and Kennedy and we walked into the building.

We stopped right near Ms. Genie's office, finding out that she was in her office. We took a few more steps until we were right behind the open door. Abree got ready to run in to get Kennedy once she got the key in case something happens. Rosemary got ready to turn into a teacher in case anything went wrong. Kennedy turned invisible and I hid behind the door with a key so that I can lock the door when we got the weapon key. Without a second to lose, Kennedy walked inside. At first all I saw was Ms. Genie working on her computer, but then I saw the box lid slowly lift up and the key floated into the air.

"What the heck? Who's there?" Ms. Genie shouted, looking intensely at the glowing key. Kennedy appeared and waved a quick smile before Abree zoomed in and the two of them shot out of there. Rosemary quickly flew behind them and I slammed the door closed. Ms. Genie ran to the door and glared at me through the window. I grinned, locked the door, and flew after them. I hurtled through the front door and Trent quickly locked the door, screaming at the others and telling them to lock their doors and run/fly to the portal.

Soon enough, the 9 of us were racing against time to get to the secret place. Shane didn't have powers, but he caught up to us as we finally got to the secret place. We pushed each other through the gap in the door and without any communication, people started to leap through the portal. Soon enough all the luggage and everyone except me and Jere were in the portal, on their way home. I looked into Jere's deep brown eyes and smiled a relaxed but forced smile. Jere smiled back and with that, we grabbed hands and jumped into the portal.

Friday, April 27, 2018.
7:02 in the morning.

The gleeful chirps of the birds and the gentle rays of light woke me up, with a more soothing alarm. I wake up, thinking I was back at the "Death Call". The events of yesterday suddenly came flooding into my mind and I looked around me in shock. I was no longer glowing cyan, and I was back in my bedroom, in my house.

"Mom! Dad! Marvin! Gale!" I screamed, springing up from my bed and running out of my room. I ran into the kitchen and saw them, my family. I beamed and cried as I ran towards them.

"Melissa? Melissa!" Marvin shouted, beaming as he ran into my arms. I squeezed him tight and lifted him into my arms. I let him go and ran to hug Gale, then my dad. I smiled and walked up to Teresa.

"I've missed you the most, mom," I said quietly. Teresa smiled and held me tight in her arms. We were all there for a moment, as a family, just like I wanted it. But without warning, I get a text from Shane.

Melissa,
Meet me at the school where we need to destroy the key. Everyone else is on their way as well. Bring your family, just in case.

See you there!
Shane

I nodded to myself and walked to the stairs leading to the upper floor, ushering them towards me.

"We'll have time to celebrate later, but for now we need to go. Get ready and I'll meet you on our front porch in 10 minutes. I'll explain on the way," I said. They nodded and raced me up the stairs and into our rooms. A few minutes later, I was explaining to them the whole situation on our quick walk to school. We met everyone at the jungle gym and after a few moments, Shane got out the key and a hammer.

"I'll just have to stop you right there, son," a familiar voice hissed behind us. We all turned around in shock at Ms. Genie standing before us. I really wanted to know how she could've possibly gotten through her locked office door, the locked building and to the portal, but I was too enraged to even consider asking. Shane walked up and pointed at her face, his finger trembling with hatred.

"You better back off, mom. You wouldn't want to mess with me in the state I'm in," Shane snarled. Ms. Genie laughed and pushed past him with ease, collecting the key as she passed him.

"I just wanted to be here as you make the worst mistake of your life and then be destroyed by me. You now have a choice, Miss Melissa. Either destroy the key and watch one of your witnesses here get hurt, or tell the court that you're my daughter and that you want me to have full custody," Ms. Genie threatened, tossing the key at me. I catch it, but immediately wanted to drop it. I have to decide between saving my school and loved ones and watch one of them get hurt, or telling the judge that I'm her daughter and that I want her to have full custody. Before I can say anything, my dad steps in.

"Amy, are you even thinking about what you're about to do?" my dad pleaded. Ms. Genie looked at him for a second, and right then and there I decided what I wanted to do. I saw in Ms. Genie's eyes hatred and greed. But in my father's eyes, I saw hope and love for the people he's fighting for. That's what I want to do, and I will be standing right next to the person who does get hurt. I get down on my knees right in front of the jungle gym, take the hammer, and slam it against the key. The key exploded and scattered all over the place, setting a light blue glow that reflected off of the jungle gym. Ms. Genie turned her attention back on me, grinning.

"Well, it looks like you've made your choice. Since I'm all about games, I'll make it a fun game. Since you destroyed the key, I get to hurt one of your colleagues here. So I'll blind all of you for a second, and I'll leave the school with the person who's getting hurt. Once you can see again, you'll have to figure out who got taken. If you can beat me to the park, I won't hurt the person. If I beat you, then they get hurt. Deal?" Ms. Genie asked. I sighed and shook her hand.

"Deal. Guys, get ready, and good luck," I breathed, glaring at her. She beamed and backed up so that she could see all of us. I ran up to Jere, Travis, and Kade and held them tight. There was suddenly a lot of dust and smoke surrounding us, making me cough uncontrollably. The dust and smoke finally went away, clearing the sky and reliving my eyes. I quickly look around. Jere and his family are all here, all of my friends and their families are still here, Shane's here, and that just leaves my family.

"Gale! Come on guys, my brother is in danger!" I suddenly yelled, floating into the sky and darting towards the park. My team followed me, picking people up who didn't have powers and taking them with us. My tears came streaming down my face and went away in seconds as the wind dried them away. I raced to the park and almost fell landing on a bench. Jere came up next to me, picked me up along with Kade and dashed towards Ms. Genie, who had Gale tied up against the basketball pole. I gasped as Ms. Genie pulled out a gun, shiny black in the early morning sky. I ran up to Ms. Genie, everyone else following.

"Mom, don't!" I whimpered, turning Ms. Genie's face to face mine, "Please, don't. Whatever is going on, we can talk about and figure it all out. Please don't kill my brother!" I cried. Ms. Genie faced me and looked at me with all of the grudge that she has always had on me. I fell to my knees and cried into my legs, unable to say anything. A few moments later, I heard the gun click in place and I shuddered in pain, even though nothing happened yet.

"Melissa, look at me," Gale whispered hoarsely. I slowly lifted my head, staring into Gale's worn out eyes and dry mouth, probably from crying and screaming.

"It's going to be ok. Take care of our family for me. I love you, Melissa," Gale murmured. I shook my head as Gale smiled and closed his eyes. Jere, Samira, Kennedy, Trent, Abree, and Lacey all tried to zoom to Gale and untie him and Amber, Belle, Rosemary, Gavin, Faye, Lucy, and I tried to fly to Gale to untie him before Ms. Genie fires, but a force bounces all of us backwards, keeping us away from the basketball hoop. I bang my fists against the force, trying to break it. I give up and with a last look at him, I reached out to him, wanting him to touch my hand one last time. Suddenly, a gunshot rang out three times.

"NO!!!!!!!!!" I screamed. The bullets shot out of the gun and two flew right into Gale's chest, one straight into his forehead. Gale's body almost immediately went limp and he smiled at me as his body fell against the pole and down into the asphalt. The force broke and I ran over to him, untying him and holding his head in my arms, warm blood pooling onto my legs.

"Gale, Gale, please don't leave me. I need you! Please don't leave me," I sobbed, bringing his head to my chest and rocking him back and forth with my grieving heart. He was dead when I placed Gale's head back on the ground, gone. I whimpered as I closed his eyelids. Marvin, dad, and Teresa we're suddenly right next to me and I leaned into them, all of us trying to hold it all in but cried anyway. I looked over at Ms. Genie and my unbearable sadness turned into despicable anger in seconds. I stood up and started to charge towards her, my pace only stopping when Jere's powerful strength held me down.

"YOU MONSTER!! YOU KILLED MY BROTHER!!!" I hollered, hot tears running down my cheeks. Ms. Genie slightly smiled and slowly walked towards me.

"Oh, I did? Well, I'm so sorry, but I believe that I'm not the monster here. You brought this on yourself. *You* killed your brother, not me," Ms. Genie smirked, turning back around and walking away. Just then, my anger boiled even more. I stood up straight and with one single motion, controlled Jere to release me. Jere's arms went slack and I flew in front of Ms. Genie.

With my insufferable heartache and all my rage in my mind, I controlled Ms. Genie to give me the gun. I breathed in slowly and within seconds the gun was pointed at her chest, my finger on the trigger. Before I knew it, the gun quickly turned to her leg and I heard gunshots yet again as I saw Ms.

Genie scream and fall to the ground. Shane, Jere, and my family walked up to me I dropped the gun, my hand shaking. I couldn't take it anymore. I started to cry and scream and tightly hug whoever was closest to me. The cops soon came and all we told them was that Ms. Genie killed my brother and then she shot herself in the leg. As we walked back home, all I could think about in my numb mind was: *How did we get here?*

Saturday, April 28, 2018.
9:30 in the morning.

I woke up crying. I woke up in a soaked bed with dark and glum clouds outside. All I could really do was sit in my bed, crying softly, holding a picture of me and Gale at our favorite place: the mountains. *At least I'm not the only one.* I thought. Teresa was sitting in her bed, sobbing over her first picture holding Gale as a baby. Marvin was screaming in his room, switching back and forth between tearing up his room and crying in the middle of the floor. Dad was slumped on the couch, watching reruns of his moments with Gale, trying his hardest not to crumple in tears.

None of us saw each other the entire day. The only person I saw today was Jere. He crept through the window and for the rest of the day we just held each other. My crying was over for the moment, probably because I was so weak. I felt like I had no purpose, like an entire limb has been chopped off or that I have been paralyzed from the neck down. The funeral was scheduled for later today. Dad said that he wanted to get the grieve over with, to say our last goodbyes before we forget to do them at all. We also decided to have Shane's adoption tomorrow. Until then, Shane is at an orphanage home.

"I don't want to go to Shane's adoption finalization, Jere," I sighed, resting my head on his shoulder. Jere nodded and started to gently rub my back, like what Gale used to do when I'm sad.

"Why not? You want Shane as your brother, right?" Jere asked. I nodded and sat up to face Jere.

"I do. But I don't want a weekend where my brother gets murdered on a Friday, his funeral on a Saturday, and then my half brother's adoption finalization on a Sunday. I feel like I'm replacing Gale, and that point is even stronger when we adopt Shane two days after he's gone," I muttered. Jere nodded and picked up a picture frame of me, Gale, Marvin, dad, and Teresa at a mini golf course.

"No one, not even Shane, can replace Gale. You know that. Gale is still here, still living right here," Jere said, pointing at my heart, "he will always be here for you. Shane is just adding on to the love you get to have throughout your life. I know Gale would love seeing you letting other people in, especially Shane," Jere slightly smiled, pulling me into a hug. I hesitated for a moment, realizing that the last person I kinda hugged was Shane. Last time I hugged anyone was when Shane was holding me back as they carried Gale away,

me trying to hold him one last time. But this hug
was different, the hug that Jere embraced me with
was with warmth and comfort. I slightly smiled as
well and stood up.

"Well, come on. We have a special funeral
to go to," I sighed. I eventually decided to wear a
laced black dress, black heels, and a diamond
infinity necklace that Gale got me for my last
birthday. Jere and I casually walked out of my
bedroom, joining the rest of my family near the front
door. None of us talked, or cried. Instead, we held
hands and walked out of the door with pride. We
were given sympathy, but none of us wanted it.

The beginning of the funeral was all in a
haze, Gale's coffin being my only focus. It wasn't
until my name was called to speak that I refocused
on what was around me. As I walked to the podium,
I could feel all eyes on me. I turned to face the
crowd and Gale's coffin, and I was already in tears.

"One of my favorite memories of Gale and I
was when we sat next to each other on Space
Mountain in Disneyland last summer. We were both
screaming and laughing at the same time as we
looked at the beautiful stars on the roller coaster
ride. I remember screaming at him, "We're living a
nightmare!" Gale grabbed my hand and yelled
back, "No we're not. We're living life!" Gale was
someone who was so optimistic, so passionate
about life and experiences. One of the only times
that he would get mad was when me or Marvin
would steal his comic collection, or when someone
didn't enjoy their life. I miss him so much, even
though the last time he smiled at me was
yesterday. I feel like a very valuable part of my

body has been ripped from me, taken to be never given back."

"But if there's one thing Gale would've wanted for me, for us to do today until forever, it is to enjoy life and live it proudly and remember that he loved us. Death leaves a heartache no one can heal, but love leaves a memory no one can steal. Rest in peace Gale, my wonderful brother and friend," I proclaimed lightly, tearing up as I walked down from the podium. I softly touched Gale's coffin and all at once, the pain and sorrow sprung back inside of me, my tears exploding in my eyes. I would've fell to the ground and cried until there were no tears left to cry if Shane and Jere didn't take my hand and lead me back to my seat. The rest of the funeral I was in tears, not knowing when I was going to stop.

It was finally time to take Gale to his grave. We walked down the gloomy sidewalks and looked at all of the other lost ones. I ended up being the last one to throw my piece of dirt unto Gale's coffin. I gradually went down to my knees and pulled out a piece of paper. It was a letter that I wrote to Gale. I kissed it, picked up a handful a dirt, and dropped both into the coffin. At that point, I didn't want to move. I stayed and watched Gale get fully buried, watched them put his tombstone in place, and watched everyone leave. It wasn't until much later that I decided to stand up and walk home to my now wounded family.

Sunday, April 29, 2018.
8:13 in the morning.

"Melissa? Melissa wake up," I hear someone distant whisper. I groaned in pain as I tried to stretch my body. My afternoon yesterday was very limited. I became very angry and started to blame random people and things for killing Gale. I had to be tied up to my bedpost inside my room for an hour to calm down. Eventually my friends came over and we watched Netflix shows to get me off obvious topics. I opened my eyes and watched Shane smile at me.

"Oh Shane, hi. Shouldn't you be getting ready for your adoption finalization?" I asked. Shane sighed and held his hands in mine. I sat up more and looked at him with concern, people who get adopted aren't usually upset.

"Yeah. It's just that, I found out your situation last night. Are you ok? Do you need me to ask to postpone my adoption?" Shane inquired. Once I heard this I jumped up and took Shane's shoulders.

"No Shane! You can't cancel or postpone your adoption. Yes, I was tied up in my room and had to watch Netflix with my friends for 3 hours in order to be distracted. But that wasn't because of you. I just, wasn't ready to let go of Gale yet. Marvin was tied up too. None of us were really ready. But I'm more than excited to have you officially be part of our family," I promised, smiling at him. Shane beamed and pulled me in for a hug.

194

"That's great, because the orphan house is awful and their food is just nasty!" Shane exclaimed. I laughed and pushed him out the room to get ready. I decided I wanted to prove to Shane that yesterday is behind me and that I'm ecstatic for him, for us, so I chose to show my inner sparkle and smile. I came out wearing a gold sparkling shirt, a pale pink blazer, and cute black jeans. Together hand in hand, the five of us walked down to court. We met up with the people that helped us throughout the entire "Death Call" journey, and together we walked in to finalize Shane's adoption.

"Before we officially finalize Shane's adoption, we would like to hear a few words from his future sister, Melissa," The judge said after all the paperwork was signed. I nodded and headed up to the witness box.

"When I first met Shane, it was all in a rush. I had just found out that my real mom was Ms. Genie that day, and a few hours later I met my half-brother. Wow! Because of all the family issues that happened those few days, I got the wrong impression of Shane. But now, I know I was wrong. Shane, he is like my twin that I have never met. He's funny, smart, talented, kind, and so much more that I have fallen in love with. He has opened up parts of me that I would've never found on my own. Shane has told me that I've shown him things that he has never experience but yet has always wanted to see."

"Both of us wanted to live our lives together as a family. So Shane, my best friend and future brother, I'm so glad and proud to welcome you to my family. We can now live together as a family like we've always wanted for the three days we've really known each other. I love you Shane, we love you. In case you were wondering, Gale also loved you too. Welcome to the fam!" I cheered, clapping my hands after I put down the mic. I wiped my tears and smiled as I walked back to the benches.

"Well, that was an amazing statement, Melissa. I couldn't have asked for a better ending. Without further to do, by the power vested in me, Shane is now officially a Logan and a part of the Logan family. Congratulations!" The judge announced. I screamed and ran over to Shane, who was standing in shock at the front desk.

I dashed into his arms and let Shane hug me close and lift me into the air. Suddenly, dad comes over and lifts both of us into the air, his happy voice booming through the courtroom. Shane and I shrieked as we flew higher and ushered Teresa and Marvin over. Teresa swooped Marvin up into her arms and rushed over to us. There we were, holding each other and celebrating the reunion that we have all always wanted, always needed. The 5 of us and our friends then went to Gale's grave, because we couldn't celebrate without him.

We made a circle around Gale's tombstone, holding hands and just feeling Gale's spirit float around us. I cried in that moment, but not because I was sad. It was because I could really fell Gale, his happiness. After a while, Marvin, dad, and mom went back home. But the rest of us stayed. I don't know exactly why all of my friends stayed, still hand in hand, but I know why I stayed. I wanted to remember Gale's heart and contagious love, I wanted to stay lost in it until part of it was truly attached to me.

But something distracted me from what I was trying to connect to. I heard something, something rustling in the delicate wind. I looked down and saw a folded piece of paper taped to the front of Gale's tombstone. *Weird, no one put a piece of paper there at the funeral*, I thought.

"Guys, look. There's is a piece of paper sticking to the tombstone," I whispered, letting go of Gavin and Lucy's hands and bending down to grab the paper. I opened it and for some reason, wasn't that surprised for what I found.

"If you thought that Gale's death and Ms. Genie possibly being in prison was the end of it, you are far from right. From the intensity of recent events, Round 2 of this "game" will be somewhere where you're families aren't, where they can't get hurt. This summer, I will be hanging out at Camp Waterfall and I would like you guys to come join me. It's not required, but here's the thing. Each of you needs something, each of you needs answers to those questions that are eating at your insides. I have those answers. Come spend the summer with me and you'll have those questions answered. Plus, it'll be lots of fun! White water rafting, rock courses, campfires with s'mores, and the ultimate challenge. Try to take down the "Death Call" before the summer's over. If you want to go, have a piece of paper in your window with your name and address on it by the end of the day on May 20th. Have a great rest of the school year and I'll see you all at Camp Waterfall! -C," We all read. I sighed and shoved the note into my wallet before I thought too deeply about it. All of us took turns giving longing and concerned looks to each other. I knew that none of us wanted to deal with this insane roller coaster, especially after Gale. But I think I speak for everyone when I say that we want this to end.

Everyone was struggling to find words for this big decision that we all had to make, but there were no words. Without any discussion, people started to leave. Shane and I were the last ones to leave.

"Well, let's do this. Ok?" I asked as calmly as possible. Shane nodded and smiled at me, putting all of his worry off to the side. I smiled as well, grabbed his hand in mine and with one last look at Gale, we turned around and walked back towards a new, crazy beginning.

That's the end of this story, for now. Who knows what will happen when summertime comes around and the time comes for all of us to decide whether to go to camp or not. Also, let's not forget C's nagging mention that we all want answers to questions that were eating at our insides, and that C had those answers. At this point I want to end this, to know the full truth that has been hiding from me for over a month.

Who is C?
Where is Ms. Genie, <u>if</u> she's not in prison?
What questions will be answered if we go?
What will we be burdened with when we get
back? What will happen before the school
year ends?

WHO AND WHERE IS THE "DEATH CALL"?

Well, I can't answer that question! You'll have to find that out with me and my team in our next story...

The Camp Signal

(Coming Soon)

THE END

About the Author

This is author M.J. Logan's first of many novels, inspired by an amazing imagination and the driving love to write. M.J. lives in her beloved Colorado and is entering her freshman year in high school in the fall of 2017. She loves to dance, read and of course, write. She hopes to change the world when she gets older and wants to makes sure her job is something she loves as an adult. Whether that is being an author or not, she isn't sure. But, either way, she hopes everyone enjoys her books!

13591086R00117

Made in the USA
San Bernardino, CA
13 December 2018